W9-CIQ-341

STEFAN ZWEIG was born in 1881 in Vienna, into a wealthy Austrian-Jewish family. He studied in Berlin and Vienna and was first known as a poet and translator, then as a biographer. Zweig travelled widely, living in Salzburg between the wars, and was an international bestseller with a string of hugely popular novellas including *Letter from an Unknown Woman*, *Amok* and *Fear*. In 1934, with the rise of Nazism, he moved to London, and later on to Bath, taking British citizenship after the outbreak of the Second World War. With the fall of France in 1940 Zweig left Britain for New York, before settling in Brazil, where in 1942 he and his wife were found dead in an apparent double suicide. Much of his work is available from Pushkin Press.

LETTER FROM AN
UNKNOWN WOMAN

AND OTHER STORIES

STEFAN ZWEIG

LETTER FROM AN UNKNOWN WOMAN

AND OTHER STORIES

Translated from the German by
Anthea Bell

PUSHKIN PRESS

LONDON

Pushkin Press
71–75 Shelton Street
London WC2H 9JQ

Original text © Williams Verlag AG Zurich
English translation © Anthea Bell

Letter from an Unknown Woman first published in German as
Brief einer Unbekannten in 1922

A Story Told in Twilight first published in German as
Geschichte in der Dämmerung in 1911

The Debt Paid Late first published in German as
Vergessene Träume in 1900

Forgotten Dreams first published in German as
Die spät bezahlte Schuld in 1982

This edition first published by Pushkin Press in 2013
ISBN 978 1 906548 93 3

Set in 11 on 15 Monotype Baskerville
by Tetragon, London
Printed and bound by CPI Group (UK) Ltd

www.pushkinpress.com

CONTENTS

LETTER FROM AN UNKNOWN WOMAN

W HEN R., *the famous novelist, returned to Vienna early in the morning, after a refreshing three-day excursion into the mountains, and bought a newspaper at the railway station, he was reminded as soon as his eye fell on the date that this was his birthday. His forty-first birthday, as he quickly reflected, an observation that neither pleased nor displeased him. He swiftly leafed through the crisp pages of the paper, and hailed a taxi to take him home to his apartment. His manservant told him that while he was away there had been two visitors as well as several telephone calls, and brought him the accumulated post on a tray. R. looked casually through it, opening a couple of envelopes because the names of their senders interested him; for the moment he set aside one letter, apparently of some length and addressed to him in writing that he did not recognize. Meanwhile the servant had brought him tea; he leant back in an armchair at his ease, skimmed the newspaper again, leafed through several other items of printed matter, then lit himself a cigar, and only now picked up the letter that he had put to one side.*

It consisted of about two dozen sheets, more of a manuscript than a letter and written hastily in an agitated, feminine hand that he did not know. He instinctively checked the envelope again in case he had

11

missed an explanatory enclosure. But the envelope was empty, and like the letter itself bore no address or signature identifying the sender. Strange, he thought, and picked up the letter once more. It began, "To you, who never knew me," which was both a salutation and a challenge. He stopped for a moment in surprise: was this letter really addressed to him or to some imaginary person? Suddenly his curiosity was aroused. And he began to read:

My child died yesterday—for three days and three nights I wrestled with death for that tender little life, I sat for forty hours at his bedside while the influenza racked his poor, hot body with fever. I put cool compresses on his forehead, I held his restless little hands day and night. On the third evening I collapsed. My eyes would not stay open any longer; I was unaware of it when they closed. I slept, sitting on my hard chair, for three or four hours, and in that time death took him. Now the poor sweet boy lies there in his narrow child's bed, just as he died; only his eyes have been closed, his clever, dark eyes, and his hands are folded over his white shirt, while four candles burn at the four corners of his bed. I dare not look, I dare not stir from my chair, for when the candles flicker shadows flit over his face and his closed mouth, and then it seems as if his features were moving, so that I might think he was not dead after all, and will wake up and say something loving and childish to me in his clear voice. But I know that he is dead, I will arm myself against hope and further disappointment, I will not look at him again. I know it is true, I know my child died yesterday—so now all I have in the world is you, you who know nothing about me, you who are now amusing yourself without a care in the world, dallying with things and with people. I have only you, who never knew me, and whom I have always loved.

I have taken the fifth candle over to the table where I am writing to you now. For I cannot be alone with my dead child without weeping my heart out, and to whom am I to speak in this terrible hour if not to you, who were and are everything to me? Perhaps I shall not be able to speak to you entirely clearly, perhaps you will not understand me—my mind is dulled, my temples throb and hammer, my limbs hurt so much. I think I am feverish myself, perhaps I too have the influenza that is spreading fast in this part of town, and I would be glad of it, because then I could go with my child without having to do myself any violence. Sometimes everything turns dark before my eyes; perhaps I shall not even be able to finish writing this letter—but I am summoning up all my strength to speak to you once, just this one time, my beloved who never knew me.

I speak only to you; for the first time I will tell you everything, the whole story of my life, a life that has always been yours although you never knew it. But you shall know my secret only once I am dead, when you no longer have to answer me, when whatever is now sending hot and cold shudders through me really is the end. If I have to live on, I shall tear this letter up and go on preserving my silence as I have always preserved it. However, if you are holding it in your hands, you will know that in these pages a dead woman is telling you the story of her life, a life that was yours from her first to her last waking hour. Do not be afraid of my words; a dead woman wants nothing any more, neither love nor pity nor comfort. I want only one thing from you: I want you to believe everything that my pain tells you here, seeking refuge with you. Believe it all, that is the only thing I ask you: no one lies in the hour of an only child's death.

I will tell you the whole story of my life, and it is a life that truly began only on the day I met you. Before that, there was nothing but murky confusion into which my memory never dipped again, some kind of cellar full of dusty, cobwebbed, sombre objects and people. My heart knows nothing about them now. When you arrived I was thirteen years old, living in the apartment building where you live now, the same building in which you are holding my letter, my last living breath, in your hands. I lived in the same corridor, right opposite the door of your apartment. I am sure you will not remember us any more, an accountant's impoverished widow (my mother always wore mourning) and her thin teenage daughter; we had quietly become imbued, so to speak, with our life of needy respectability. Perhaps you never even heard our name, because we had no nameplate on the front door of our apartment, and no one came to visit us or asked after us. And it is all so long ago, fifteen or sixteen years; no, I am sure you don't remember anything about it, my beloved, but I—oh, I recollect every detail with passion. As if it were today, I remember the very day, no, the very hour when I first heard your voice and set eyes on you for the first time, and how could I not? It was only then that the world began for me. Allow me, beloved, to tell you the whole story from the beginning. I beg you, do not tire of listening to me for a quarter of an hour, when I have never tired of loving you all my life.

Before you moved into our building a family of ugly, mean-minded, quarrelsome people lived behind the door of your apartment. Poor as they were, what they hated most was the poverty next door, ours, because we wanted nothing to do with their down-at-heel, vulgar, uncouth manners. The man was a drunk and beat his wife; we were often woken in the night by the noise of chairs falling over and plates breaking; and once the wife, bruised and bleeding, her hair all tangled, ran out onto the stairs with the drunk shouting abuse after her until the neighbours came out of their own doors and threatened him with the police. My mother avoided any contact with that couple from the first, and forbade me to speak to their children, who seized every opportunity of avenging themselves on me. When they met me in the street they called me dirty names, and once threw such hard snowballs at me that I was left with blood running from my forehead. By some common instinct, the whole building hated that family, and when something suddenly happened to them—I think the husband was jailed for theft—and they had to move out, bag and baggage, we all breathed a sigh of relief. A few days later the "To Let" notice was up at the entrance of the building, and then it was taken down; the caretaker let it be known—and word quickly went around—that a single, quiet gentleman, a writer, had taken the apartment. That was when I first heard your name.

In a few days' time painters and decorators, wallpaper-hangers and cleaners came to remove all trace of the apartment's previous grubby owners; there was much knocking and hammering, scraping and scrubbing, but my mother was glad of it. At last, she said, there would be an end to the sloppy housekeeping in that apartment. I still had not come face to face with you by the time you moved in; all this work was supervised by your manservant, that small, serious, grey-haired gentleman's gentleman, who directed operations in his quiet, objective, superior way. He impressed us all very much, first because a gentleman's gentleman was something entirely new in our suburban apartment building, and then because he was so extremely civil to everyone, but without placing himself on a par with the other servants and engaging them in conversation as one of themselves. From the very first day he addressed my mother with the respect due to a lady, and he was always gravely friendly even to me, little brat that I was. When he mentioned your name he did so with a kind of special esteem—anyone could tell at once that he thought far more of you than a servant usually does of his master. And I liked him so much for that, good old Johann, although I envied him for always being with you to serve you.

16

I am telling you all this, beloved, all these small and rather ridiculous things, so that you will understand how you could have such power, from the first, over the shy, diffident child I was at the time. Even before you yourself came into my life, there was an aura around you redolent of riches, of something out of the ordinary, of mystery— all of us in that little suburban apartment building were waiting impatiently for you to move in (those who live narrow lives are always curious about any novelty on their doorsteps). And how strongly I, above all, felt that curiosity to see you when I came home from school one afternoon and saw the removals van standing outside the building. The men had already taken in most of the furniture, the heavy pieces, and now they were carrying up a few smaller items; I stayed standing by the doorway so that I could marvel at everything, because all your possessions were so interestingly different from anything I had ever seen before. There were Indian idols, Italian sculptures, large pictures in very bright colours, and then, finally, came the books, so many of them, and more beautiful than I would ever have thought possible. They were stacked up by the front door of the apartment, where the manservant took charge of them, carefully knocking the dust off every single volume with a stick and a feather duster. I prowled curiously around the ever-growing pile, and the manservant did not tell me to go away, but he didn't encourage me either, so I dared not touch one, although I would have loved to feel the soft leather of many of their bindings. I only glanced shyly and surreptitiously at the titles; there

17

were French and English books among them, and many in languages that I didn't know. I think I could have stood there for hours looking at them all, but then my mother called me in.

After that, I couldn't stop thinking of you all evening, and still I didn't know you. I myself owned only a dozen cheap books with shabby board covers, but I loved them more than anything and read them again and again. And now I couldn't help wondering what the man who owned and had read all these wonderful books must be like, a man who knew so many languages, who was so rich and at the same time so learned. There was a kind of supernatural awe in my mind when I thought of all those books. I tried to picture you: you were an old man with glasses and a long white beard, rather like our geography teacher, only much kinder, better-looking and better-tempered—I don't know why I already felt sure you must be good-looking, when I still thought of you as an old man. All those years ago, that was the first night I ever dreamt of you, and still I didn't know you.

You moved in yourself the next day, but for all my spying I hadn't managed to catch a glimpse of you yet—which only heightened my curiosity. At last, on the third day, I did see you, and what a surprise it was to find you so different, so wholly unrelated to my childish image of someone resembling God the Father. I had dreamt of a kindly, bespectacled old man, and now here you were— exactly the same as you are today. You are proof against change, the years slide off you! You wore a casual fawn suit, and ran upstairs in your incomparably light, boyish way, always taking two steps at a time. You were carrying your hat, so I saw, with indescribable amazement, your bright, lively face and youthful head of hair; I was truly amazed to find how young, how handsome, how supple, slender and elegant you were. And isn't it strange? In that first second I clearly felt what I, like everyone else, am surprised to find is a unique trait in your character: somehow you are two men at once: one a hot-blooded young man who takes life easily, delighting in games and adventure, but at the same time, in your art, an implacably serious man, conscious of your duty, extremely well read and highly educated. I unconsciously sensed, again like everyone else, that you lead a double life, one side of it bright and open to the world, the other very dark, known to you alone—my thirteen-year-old self, magically attracted to you at first glance, was aware of that profound duality, the secret of your nature.

Do you understand now, beloved, what a miracle, what an enticing enigma you were bound to seem to me as a child? A man whom I revered because he wrote books, because he was famous in that other great world, and suddenly I found out that he was an elegant, boyishly cheerful young man of twenty-five! Need I tell you that from that day on nothing at home, nothing in my entire impoverished childhood world interested me except for you, that with all the doggedness, all the probing persistence of a thirteen-year-old I thought only of you and your life. I observed you, I observed your habits and the people who visited you, and my curiosity

19

about you was increased rather than satisfied, because the duality of your nature was expressed in the wide variety of those visitors. Young people came, friends of yours with whom you laughed in high spirits, lively students, and then there were ladies who drove up in cars, once the director of the opera house, that great conductor whom I had only ever seen from a reverent distance on his rostrum, then again young girls still at commercial college who scurried shyly in through your door, and women visitors in particular, very, very many women. I thought nothing special of that, not even when, on my way to school one morning, I saw a heavily veiled lady leave your apartment—I was only thirteen, after all, and the passionate curiosity with which I spied on your life and lay in wait for you did not, in the child, identify itself as love.

But I still remember, my beloved, the day and the hour when I lost my heart to you entirely and for ever. I had been for a walk with a school friend, and we two girls were standing at the entrance to the building, talking, when a car drove up, stopped—and you jumped off the running-board with the impatient, agile gait that still fascinates me in you. An instinctive urge came over me to open the door for you, and so I crossed your path and we almost collided. You looked at me with a warm, soft, all-enveloping gaze that was like a caress, smiled at me tenderly—yes, I can put it no other way—and said in a low and almost intimate tone of voice: "Thank you very much, Fräulein."

That was all, beloved, but from that moment on, after sensing that soft, tender look, I was your slave. I learnt later, in fact quite soon, that you look in the same way at every woman you encounter, every shop girl who sells you something, every housemaid who opens the door to you, with an all-embracing expression that surrounds and yet at the same time undresses a woman, the look of the born seducer; and that glance of yours is not a deliberate expression of will and inclination, but you are entirely unconscious that your tenderness to women makes them feel warm and soft when it is turned on them. However, I did not guess that at the age of thirteen, still a child; it was as if I had been immersed in fire. I thought the tenderness was only for me, for me alone, and in that one second the woman latent in my adolescent self awoke, and she was in thrall to you for ever.

"Who was that?" asked my friend. I couldn't answer her at once. It was impossible for me to utter your name; in that one single second it had become sacred to me, it was my secret. "Oh, a gentleman who lives in this building," I stammered awkwardly at last. "Then why did you blush like that when he looked at you?" my friend mocked me, with all the malice of an inquisitive child. And because I felt her touching on my secret with derision, the blood rose to my cheeks more warmly than ever. My embarrassment made me snap at her. "You silly goose!" I said angrily; I could have throttled her. But she just laughed even louder, yet more scornfully, until I felt the tears shoot to my eyes with helpless rage. I left her standing there and ran upstairs.

I loved you from that second on. I know that women have often said those words to you, spoilt as you are. But believe me, no one ever loved you as slavishly, with such dog-like devotion, as the creature I was then and have always remained, for there is nothing on earth like the love of a child that passes unnoticed in the dark because she has no hope: her love is so submissive, so much a servant's love, passionate and lying in wait, in a way that the avid yet unconsciously demanding love of a grown woman can never be. Only lonely children can keep a passion entirely to themselves; others talk about their feelings in company, wear them away in intimacy with friends, they have heard and read a great deal about love, and know that it is a common fate. They play with it as if it were a toy, they show it off like boys smoking their first cigarette. But as for me, I had no one I could take into my confidence, I was not taught or warned by anyone, I was inexperienced and naive; I flung myself into my fate as if into an abyss. Everything growing and emerging in me knew of nothing but you, the dream of you was my familiar friend. My father had died long ago, my mother was a stranger to me in her eternal sad depression, her anxious pensioner's worries; more knowing adolescent schoolgirls repelled me because they played so lightly with what to me was the ultimate passion—so with all the concentrated attention of my impatiently emergent nature I brought to bear, on you, everything that would otherwise have been splintered and dispersed. To me, you were—how can I put it? Any one comparison is too slight—you were everything to me, all that mattered. Nothing existed except in so far as it related to you, you were the only point of reference in my life.

You changed it entirely. Before, I had been an indifferent pupil at school, and my work was only average; now I was suddenly top of the class, I read a thousand books until late into the night because I knew that you loved books; to my mother's amazement I suddenly began practising the piano with stubborn persistence because I thought you also loved music. I cleaned and mended my clothes solely to look pleasing and neat in front of you, and I hated the fact that my old school pinafore (a house dress of my mother's cut down to size) had a square patch on the left side of it. I was afraid you might notice the patch and despise me, so I always kept my school bag pressed over it as I ran up the stairs, trembling with fear in case you saw it. How foolish of me: you never, or almost never, looked at me again.

And yet I really did nothing all day but wait for you and look out for you. There was a small brass peephole in our door, and looking through its circular centre I could see your door opposite. This peephole—no, don't smile, beloved, even today I am still not ashamed of those hours!—was my eye on the world. I sat in the cold front room, afraid of my mother's suspicions, on the watch for whole afternoons in those months and years, with a book in my hand, tense as a musical string resounding in response to your presence. I was always looking out for you, always in a state of tension, but you felt it as little as the tension of the spring in the watch that you carry in your pocket, patiently counting and measuring your hours in the dark, accompanying your movements with its inaudible heartbeat, while you let your quick glance fall on it only once in a million ticking seconds. I knew everything about you, knew all your habits, every one of your suits and ties, I knew your various acquaintances and could soon tell them apart, dividing them into those whom I liked and those whom I didn't; from my thirteenth to my sixteenth year I lived every hour for you. Oh, what follies I committed! I kissed the door handle that your hand had touched; I stole a cigarette end that you had dropped before coming into the building, and it was sacred to me because your lips had touched it. In the evenings I would run down to the street a hundred times on some pretext or other to see which of your rooms had a light in it, so that I could feel more aware of your invisible presence. And in the weeks when you went away—my heart always missed a beat in anguish when I saw your good manservant Johann carrying your yellow travelling bag downstairs—in those weeks my life was dead and pointless. I went about feeling morose, bored and cross, and I always had to take care that my mother did not notice the despair in my red-rimmed eyes.

Even as I tell you all these things, I know that they were grotesquely extravagant and childish follies. I ought to have been ashamed of them, but I was not, for my love for you was never purer and more passionate than in those childish excesses. I could tell you for hours, days, how I lived with you at that time, and you hardly even knew me by sight, because if I met you on the stairs and there was no avoiding it, I would run past you with my head bent for fear of your burning gaze—like someone plunging into water—just to escape being scorched by its fire. For hours, days I could tell you about those long-gone years of yours, unrolling the whole calendar of your life, but I do not mean to bore you or torment you. I will tell you only about the best experience of my childhood, and I ask you not to mock me because it is something so slight, for to me as a child it was infinite. It must have been on a Sunday. You had gone away, and your servant was dragging the heavy carpets that he had been beating back through the open front door of the apartment. It was hard work for the good man, and in a suddenly bold moment I went up to him and asked if I could help him. He was surprised, but let me do as I suggested, and so I saw—if only I could tell you with what reverent, indeed devout veneration!—I saw your apartment from the inside, your world, the desk where you used to sit, on which a few flowers stood in a blue crystal vase. Your cupboards, your pictures, your books. It was only a fleeting, stolen glimpse of your life, for the faithful Johann would certainly not have let me look closely, but with that one glimpse I took in the whole atmosphere, and now I had nourishment for never-ending dreams of you both waking and sleeping.

That brief moment was the happiest of my childhood. I wanted to tell you about it so that even though you do not know me you may get some inkling of how my life depended on you. I wanted to tell you about that, and about the terrible moment that was, unfortunately, so close to it. I had—as I have already told you—forgotten everything but you, I took no notice of my mother any more, or indeed of anyone else. I hardly noticed an elderly gentleman, a businessman from Innsbruck who was distantly related to my mother by marriage, coming to visit us often and staying for some time; indeed, I welcomed his visits, because then he sometimes took Mama to the theatre, and I could be on my own, thinking of you, looking out for you, which was my greatest and only bliss. One day my mother called me into her room with a certain ceremony, saying she had something serious to discuss with me. I went pale and suddenly heard my heart thudding; did she suspect something, had she guessed? My first thought was of you, the secret that linked me to the world. But my mother herself was ill at ease; she kissed me affectionately once, and then again (as she never usually did), drew me down on the sofa beside her and began to tell me, hesitantly and bashfully, that her relation, who was a widower, had made her a proposal of marriage, and mainly for my sake she had decided to accept him. The hot blood rose to my heart: I had only one thought in answer to what she said, the thought of you.

"But we'll be staying here, won't we?" I just managed to stammer.

"No, we're moving to Innsbruck. Ferdinand has a lovely villa there."

I heard no more. Everything went black before my eyes. Later, I knew that I had fallen down in a faint; I heard my mother, her voice lowered, quietly telling my prospective stepfather, who had been waiting outside the door, that

I had suddenly stepped back with my hands flung out, and then I fell to the floor like a lump of lead. I cannot tell you what happened in the next few days, how I, a powerless child, tried to resist my mother's all-powerful will; as I write, my hand still trembles when I think of it. I could not give my real secret away, so my resistance seemed like mere obstinacy, malice and defiance. No one spoke to me, it was all done behind my back. They used the hours when I was at school to arrange our move; when I came back, something else had always been cleared away or sold. I saw our home coming apart, and my life with it, and one day when I came in for lunch, the removals men had been to pack everything and take it all away. Our packed suitcases stood in the empty rooms, with two camp beds for my mother and me; we were to sleep there one more night, the last, and then travel to Innsbruck the next day.

On that last day I felt, with sudden resolution, that I could not live without being near you. I knew of nothing but you that could save me. I shall never be able to say what I was thinking of, or whether I was capable of thinking clearly at all in those hours of despair, but suddenly—my mother was out—I stood up in my school clothes, just as I was, and walked across the corridor to your apartment. Or rather, I did not so much walk; it was more as if, with my stiff legs and trembling joints, I was magnetically attracted to your door. As I have said before, I had no clear idea what I wanted. Perhaps to fall at your feet and beg you to keep me as a maidservant, a slave, and I am

27

afraid you will smile at this innocent devotion on the part of a fifteen-year-old, but—beloved, you would not smile if you knew how I stood out in that ice-cold corridor, rigid with fear yet impelled by an incomprehensible power, and how I forced my trembling arm away from my body so that it rose and—after a struggle in an eternity of terrible seconds—placed a finger on the bell-push by the door handle and pressed it. To this day I can hear its shrill ringing in my ears, and then the silence afterwards when my blood seemed to stop flowing, and I listened to find out if you were coming.

But you did not come. No one came. You were obviously out that afternoon, and Johann must have gone shopping, so with the dying sound of the bell echoing in my ears I groped my way back to our destroyed, emptied apartment and threw myself down on a plaid rug, as exhausted by the four steps I had taken as if I had been trudging through deep snow for hours. But underneath that exhaustion my determination to see you, to speak to you before they tore me away, was still burning as brightly as ever. There was, I swear it, nothing sensual in my mind; I was still ignorant, for the very reason that I thought of nothing but you. I only wanted to see you, see you once more, cling to you. I waited for you all night, beloved, all that long and terrible night. As soon as my mother had got into bed and fallen asleep I slipped into the front room, to listen for your footsteps when you came home. I waited all night, and it was icy January weather. I was tired, my limbs hurt, and there was no armchair left in the room for me to sit in, so I lay down flat on the cold floor, in the draught that came in under the door. I lay on the painfully cold floor in nothing but my thin dress all night, for I took no blanket with me; I did not want to be warm for fear of falling asleep and failing to hear your step. It hurt; I got cramp in my feet, my arms were shaking; I had to keep standing up, it was so cold in that dreadful darkness. But I waited and waited and waited for you, as if for my fate.

At last—it must have been two or three in the morning—I heard the front door of the building being unlocked down below, and then footsteps coming upstairs. The cold had left me as if dropping away, heat shot through me; I quietly opened the door to rush towards you and fall at your feet… oh, I don't know what I would have done, such a foolish child as I was then. The steps came closer and closer, I saw the flicker of candlelight. Shaking, I clung to the door handle. Was it you coming?

Yes. It was you, beloved—but you were not alone. I heard a soft, provocative laugh, the rustle of a silk dress, and your lowered voice—you were coming home with a woman…

How I managed to survive that night I do not know. Next morning, at eight o'clock, they dragged me off to Innsbruck; I no longer had the strength to resist.

My child died last night—and now I shall be alone again, if I must really go on living. They will come tomorrow, strange, hulking, black-clad men bringing a coffin, and they will put him in it, my poor boy, my only child. Perhaps

29

friends will come as well, bringing flowers, but what do flowers on a coffin mean? They will comfort me, and say this and that—words, words, how can they help me? I know that I must be alone again when they have gone. I felt it then, in those two endless years in Innsbruck, the years from my sixteenth to my eighteenth birthday, when I lived like a prisoner or an outcast in my family. My stepfather, a very placid, taciturn man, was kind to me; my mother seemed ready to grant all my wishes, as if atoning for her unwitting injustice to me; young people tried to make friends with me, but I rejected all their advances with passionate defiance. I didn't want to live happy and content away from you, I entrenched myself in a dark world of self-torment and loneliness. I didn't wear the brightly coloured new clothes they bought me, I refused to go to concerts or the theatre, or on outings in cheerful company. I hardly went out at all: would you believe it, beloved, I didn't come to know more than ten streets of the little town in the two years I lived there? I was in mourning, and I wanted to mourn, I became intoxicated by every privation that I imposed on myself over and beyond the loss of you. And I did not want to be distracted from my passion to live only for you. I stayed at home alone for hours, days, doing nothing but thinking of you again and again, always reviving my hundred little memories of you, every time I met you, every time I waited for you, staging those little incidents in my mind as if in a theatre. And that is why, because I went over every second of the past countless times, I retain such a vivid memory of my whole childhood that I feel every minute of those past years with as much heat and ardour as if they were only yesterday.

My life at the time was lived entirely through you. I bought all your books; when your name was in the news-paper it was a red-letter day. Would you believe that I know every line of your books by heart, I have read them so often? If anyone were to wake me from sleep at night and quote a random line from them, I could still, thirteen years later, go on reciting the text from there, as if in a dream: every word of yours was my Gospel and prayer book. The whole world existed only in relation to you; I read about concerts and premieres in the Viennese newspapers with the sole aim of wondering which of them might interest you, and when evening came I was with you, even though I was so far away: now he is going into the auditorium, now he is sitting down. I dreamt of that a thousand times because I had once seen you at a concert.

But why describe this raving, tragic, hopeless devotion on the part of an abandoned child feeling angry with herself, why describe it to a man who never guessed at it or knew about it? Yet was I really still a child at that time? I reached the age of seventeen, eighteen—young men turned to look at me in the street, but that only embittered me. To love, or even merely play at love with anyone but you was so inexplicable to me, so unimaginably strange an idea, that merely feeling tempted to indulge in it would have seemed to me a crime. My passion for you was the same as ever, except that my body was changing, and now that my senses were awakened it was more glowing, physical, womanly. And what the child with her sombre, untaught will, the child who had pressed your doorbell, could not guess at was now my only thought: to give myself to you, devote myself to you.

The people around me thought me timid, called me shy (I had kept my secret strictly to myself). But I was developing an iron will. All that I thought and did tended in one direction: back to Vienna, back to you. And I imposed my will by force, senseless and extraordinary as it might seem to anyone else. My stepfather was a prosperous man, and regarded me as his own child. But I insisted, with grim obstinacy, that I wanted to earn my own living, and at last I managed to get a position with a relation as an assistant in a large ready-to-wear dress shop.

Need I tell you where I went first when I arrived back in Vienna—at last, at last!—one misty autumn evening? I left my case at the station, boarded a tram—how slowly it seemed to be going, I bitterly resented every stop—and hurried to the apartment building. There was light in your windows; my whole heart sang. Only now did the city, strange to me these days with its pointless roar of traffic, come to life, only now did I come to life again myself, knowing that I was near you, you, my only dream. I did not guess that in reality I was as far from your mind now, when only the thin, bright glass pane stood between you and my radiant gaze, as if valleys, mountains and rivers separated us. I merely looked up and up; there was light there, here was the building, and there were you, the whole world to me. I had dreamt of this hour for two years, and

32

now I was granted it. I stood outside your windows all that long, mild, cloudy evening, until the light in them went out. Only then did I go home to the place where I was staying.

Every evening after that I stood outside your building in the same way. I worked in the shop until six; it was hard, strenuous work, but I liked it, because all the activity there made me feel my own restlessness less painfully. And as soon as the iron shutters rolled down behind me I hurried to my desired destination. My will was set on seeing you just once, meeting you just once, so that my eyes could see your face again, if only from a distance. And after about a week it finally happened: I met you at a moment when I didn't expect it. Just as I was looking up at your windows, you came across the street. Suddenly I was that thirteen-year-old child again, and felt the blood rise to my cheeks. Instinctively, against my innermost urge to feel your eyes on me, I lowered my head and hurried past you, quick as lightning. Afterwards I was ashamed of my timid flight, the reaction of a schoolgirl, for now I knew very clearly what I wanted: I wanted to meet you, I was seeking you out, I wanted you to recognize me after all those years of weary longing, wanted you to take some notice of me, wanted you to love me.

But it was a long time before you really noticed me, although I stood out in your street every evening, even in flurries of snow and the keen, cutting wind of Vienna. I often waited in vain for hours, and often, in the end, you left the building in the company of friends. Twice I saw you

33

with women, and now that I was an adult I sensed what was new and different about my feeling for you from the sudden tug at my heartstrings, wrenching them right apart, when I saw a strange woman walking so confidently arm in arm with you. I was not surprised. After all, I knew about your succession of women visitors from my childhood days, but now it hurt me physically, and I was torn between hostility and desire in the face of your obvious intimacy with someone else. One day, childishly proud as I was and perhaps still am, I stayed away from your building, but what a terrible, empty evening of defiance and rebellion I spent! Next evening, once again, I was standing humbly outside your building waiting, waiting, just as I had spent my whole life standing outside your life, which was closed to me.

And at last one evening you did notice me. I had already seen you coming in the distance, and I steeled my will not to avoid you. As chance would have it, a cart waiting to be unloaded obstructed the street, and you had to pass close to me. Involuntarily your absent-minded gaze fell on me, and as soon as it met the attention of my own eyes—oh, what a shock the memory gave me!—it became that look you give women, the tender, all-enveloping, all-embracing gaze that also strips them, the look that, when I was a child, had made me into a loving woman for the first time. For one or two seconds that gaze held mine, which neither could nor wished to tear itself away—and then you had passed me. My heart was beating fast; instinctively I slowed my pace, and as I turned, out of a curiosity that I could not master, I saw that you too had stopped and were still looking at

34

me. And the way you observed me, with such interest and curiosity, told me at once that you did not recognize me.

You did not recognize me, neither then nor ever, you never recognized me. How can I describe to you, beloved, the disappointment of that moment? That was the first time I suffered it, the disappointment of going unrecognized by you. I have lived with it all my life, I am dying with it, and still you do not recognize me. How can I make you understand my disappointment? During those two years in Innsbruck, when I thought of you every hour and did nothing but imagine our next meeting back in Vienna, I had dreamt of the wildest—or the most blissful—possibilities, depending on my mood at the time. I had dreamt, if I may so put it, of everything; in dark moments I had pictured you rejecting me, despising me for being too uninteresting, too ugly, too importunate. In passionate visions I had gone through all forms of your disfavour, your coldness, your indifference—but in no moment of dark emotion, not even in full awareness of my inferiority, had I ventured to envisage this, the worst thing of all: the fact that you had never even noticed my existence. Today I understand it— ah, you have taught me to understand it!—I realize that, to a man, a girl's or a woman's face must have something extraordinarily changeable in it, because it is usually only a mirror reflecting now passion, now childishness, now weariness, and passes by as a reflection does; so that a man can easily forget a woman's face because age changes its light and shade, and different clothes give her a new setting. Those who are resigned to their fate really know that. However, still a girl at the time, I could not yet grasp your forgetfulness, because somehow my immoderate, constant concern with you had made me feel—although it was a delusion—that you, too, must often think of me, you would be waiting for me; how could I have gone on breathing in the certainty that I was nothing to you, no memory of me ever touched you, however lightly? And this moment, when your eyes showed me that nothing in you recognized me, no thin gossamer line of memory reached from your life to mine, was my first fall into the depths of reality, my first inkling of my destiny.

You did not recognize me at that time. And when, two days later, we met again, your eyes rested on me with a certain familiarity, you still did not recognize me as the girl who loved you and whom you had woken to life, but only as the pretty eighteen-year-old who had met you in the same place two days earlier. You looked at me in surprise, but in a friendly manner, with a slight smile playing round your mouth. Once again you passed me, once again immediately slowing your pace; I trembled, I rejoiced, I prayed that you would speak to me. I felt that, for the first time, you saw me as a living woman; I myself slowed down and did not avoid you. And suddenly I sensed you behind me; without turning round I knew that now, for the first time, I would hear your beloved voice speaking directly to me. Expectation paralysed me; I feared I would have to stop where I was because my heart was thudding so violently—and then you were beside me. You spoke to me in your easy, cheerful way, as if we had been on friendly terms for a long time—oh, you had no idea about me, you have never had any idea of my life!—so captivatingly free and easy was the way you spoke to me that I was even able to answer you. We walked all down the street side by side. Then you suggested that we might go and have something to eat together. I agreed. What would I ever have dared to deny you?

We ate together in a small restaurant—do you still know where it was? No, I am sure you don't distinguish it now from other such evenings, for who was I to you? One among hundreds, one adventure in an ever-continuing chain. And what was there for you to remember about me? I said little, because it made me so infinitely happy to have you near me, to hear you speaking to me. I did not want to waste a moment of it by asking questions or saying something foolish. I shall never forget my gratitude to you for that hour, or how entirely you responded to my passionate reverence, how tender, light and tactful you were, entirely without making importunate advances, entirely without any hasty, caressing gestures of affection, and from the first moment striking a note of such certain and friendly familiarity that you would have won my heart even if it had not been yours long ago, given with all my goodwill. Ah, you have no idea what a wonderful thing you did in not disappointing my five years of childish expectation!

It was getting late; we left the restaurant. At the door you asked me whether I was in a hurry or still had time to spare. How could I have failed to show that I was ready for you? I said that I could indeed spare some time. Then you asked,

37

quickly surmounting a slight hesitation, whether I would like to go to your apartment and talk. "Oh, most happily," I said, and it came out of the fullness of my feelings so naturally that I noticed at once how you reacted, in either embarrassment or pleasure, to my quick tongue—but you were also visibly surprised. Today I understand why you were astonished; I know it is usual for women, even when they long to give themselves, to deny that readiness, pretending to be alarmed or indignant, so that first they have to be reassured by urgent pleading, lies, vows and promises. I know that perhaps only prostitutes, the professionals of love, or perhaps very naive adolescents, respond to such an invitation with such wholehearted, joyful consent as mine. But in me—and how could you guess that?—it was only my will put into words, the concentrated longing of a thousand days breaking out. In any case, you were struck; I began to interest you. I sensed that, as we were walking along, you glanced sideways at me with a kind of astonishment while we talked. Your feelings, your magically sure sense of all that is human, immediately scented something unusual here, a secret in this pretty, compliant girl. Your curiosity was awakened, and I noticed, from your circling, probing questions, that you wanted to discover the mystery. But I evaded you; it would be better to seem foolish than to let you know my secret.

We went up to your apartment. Forgive me, beloved, when I tell you that you cannot understand what that corridor, that staircase meant to me—what turmoil and confusion there was in my mind, what headlong, painful, almost mortal happiness. Even now I can hardly think of it without tears, and I have none of those left. But imagine that every object in the building was, so to speak, imbued with my passion, each was a symbol of my childhood, my longing: the gate where I had waited for you thousands of times, the stairs from which I always listened for your footsteps, and where I had seen you for the first time, the peephole through which I had stared my soul out, the doormat outside your door where I had once knelt, the click of the key at which I had always leapt up from where I was lying in wait. All my childhood, all my passion were here in those few metres of space; this was my whole life, and now it came over me like a storm, everything, everything was coming true, and I was with you, going into your, into our apartment building. Think of it—it sounds banal, but I can't put it any other way—as if going only as far as your door had been my reality all my life, my sombre everyday world, but beyond it a child's magic realm began, the realm of Aladdin, remember that I had stared a thousand times, with burning eyes, at the door through which I now stepped, almost reeling, and you will guess—but only guess, you can never entirely know, beloved!—what that tumultuous minute meant in my life.

I stayed with you all night. You did not realize that no man had ever touched me before, had ever felt or seen my body. But how could you guess that, beloved, when I offered no resistance, showed no bashful hesitancy, so that you could have no idea of my secret love for you? It would certainly have alarmed you, for you love only what is light and playful, weightless, you are afraid of intervening in someone else's life. You want to give of yourself to everyone, to the world, but you do not want sacrificial victims. If I tell you now, beloved, that I was a virgin when I gave myself to you, I beg you not to misunderstand me! I am not accusing you, you did not entice me, lie to me, seduce me—it was I who pressed myself on you, threw myself on your breast and into my own fate. I will never, never blame you for anything, I will only thank you for the richness of that night, sparkling with desire, hovering in bliss. When I opened my eyes in the dark and felt you at my side, I was surprised not to see the stars above me, I could feel heaven so close—no, I never regretted it, beloved, for the sake of that hour I never regretted it. I remember that when you were asleep and I heard your breathing, felt your body, while I was so close to you, I shed tears of happiness in the dark.

In the morning I was in a hurry to leave early. I had to go to the shop, and I also wanted to be gone before your manservant arrived; I couldn't have him seeing me. When I was dressed and stood in front of you, you took me in your arms and gave me a long look; was some dark and distant memory stirring in you, or did I merely seem to you beautiful, happy as indeed I was? Then you kissed me on the mouth. I gently drew away, about to go. "Won't you take a few flowers with you?" you asked, and I said yes. You took four white roses out of the blue crystal vase on the desk (which I knew from that one stolen childhood glance) and gave them to me. I was still kissing them days later.

We had arranged to meet again another evening. I went, and again it was wonderful. You gave me a third night. Then you said you had to go away—oh, how I hated those journeys of yours even in my childhood!—and promised to get in touch with me as soon as you were back. I gave you a poste restante address. I didn't want to tell you my name. I kept my secret. And again you gave me a few roses when you said goodbye—goodbye.

Every day for two whole months I went to ask if any post had come… but no, why describe the hellish torment of waiting, why describe my despair to you? I am not blaming you, I love you as the man you are, hot-blooded and forgetful, ardent and inconstant, I love you just as you always were and as you still are. You had come back long ago, I could tell that by the light in your windows, and you did not write to me. I have not had a line from you to this day and these last hours of mine, not a line from you to whom I gave my life. I waited, I waited in despair. But you did not get in touch with me, you never wrote me a line… not a line…

My child died yesterday—he was also yours. He was your child, beloved, conceived on one of those three nights, I swear it, and no one tells lies in the shadow of death. He was our child, and I swear it to you, because no man touched me between those hours when I gave myself to you and the time when he made his way out of my body. I was sacred to myself because of your touch; how could

41

I have shared myself with you, who had been everything to me, and other men who passed by touching my life only slightly? He was our child, beloved, the child of my conscious love and your careless, passing, almost unconscious affection, our child, our son, our only child. You will ask—perhaps alarmed, perhaps only surprised—you will ask, beloved, why I kept the child secret all these long years, and mention him only today, now that he lies here sleeping in the dark, sleeping for ever, ready to leave and never return, never again? But how could I have told you? You would never have believed me, a stranger who showed herself only too willing on those three nights, who gave herself to you without resistance, indeed with desire, you would never have believed the anonymous woman of your fleeting encounter if she said she was keeping faith with you, the faithless—you would never have considered the child your own without suspicion! Even if what I said had seemed probable to you, you would never have been able to dismiss the secret suspicion that I was trying to palm off some other man's child on you because you were prosperous. You would have suspected me, a shadow would have remained, a fugitive, tentative shadow of distrust between us. I didn't want that. And then I know you; I know you rather better than you know yourself. I know that it would have been difficult for you, who love the carefree, light-hearted, playful aspect of love, suddenly to be a father, suddenly responsible for someone else's life. You can breathe only at liberty; you would have felt bound to me in some way. You would have hated me for that—I know that you would have done so, against your own conscious will. Perhaps only for hours, perhaps only for fleeting minutes I would have been a burden to you, a hated burden—but in my pride I wanted you to think of me all your life without any anxiety. I preferred to take it all on myself rather than burden you, I wanted to be the only one among all your women of whom you always thought with love and gratitude. But the fact is that you never thought of me at all, you forgot me.

I am not blaming you, my beloved, no, I am not blaming you. Forgive me if a touch of bitterness flows into my pen now and then, forgive me—my child, our child lies dead in the flickering candlelight; I clenched my fists against God and called him a murderer, my senses are confused and dulled. Forgive my lament, forgive me! I know that deep in your heart you are good and helpful, you help everyone, even a total stranger who asks for help. But your kindness is so strange, it is open to all to take as much of it as they can hold, it is great, infinitely great, your kindness, but it is—forgive me—it is passive. It wants to be appealed to, to be taken. You help when you are called upon to help, when you are asked for help, you help out of shame, out of weakness, and not out of joy. You do not—let me say so openly—you do not like those who are in need and torment any better than their happier brothers. And it is hard to ask anything of people like you, even the kindest of them. Once, when I was still a child looking through the peephole in our door, I saw you give something to a beggar who had rung your bell. You gave him money

43

readily before he asked you, even a good deal of it, but you gave it with a certain anxiety and in haste, wanting him to go away again quickly; it was as if you were afraid to look him in the face. I have never forgotten your uneasy, timid way of helping, fleeing from gratitude. And so I never turned to you. Certainly I know that you would have stood by me then, even without any certainty that the child was yours. You would have comforted me, you would have given me money, plenty of money, but never with anything but a secret impatience to push what was unwelcome away from you; yes, I believe you might even have asked me to do away with the child before its birth. And I feared that more than anything—because what would I not have done if you wanted it, how could I have denied you anything? However, that child meant everything to me, because it was yours, yourself again but no longer as a happy, carefree man whom I could not hold, yourself given to me for ever—so I thought—there in my body, a part of my own life. Now at last I had caught you, I could sense your life growing in my veins, I could give you food and drink, caress and kiss you when my heart burned for that. You see, beloved, that is why I was so blissfully happy when I knew that I was carrying a child of yours, that is why I never told you, because then you could not escape from me again.

To be sure, beloved, they were not such blissful months as I had anticipated in my mind, they were also months of horror and torment, of revulsion at the vileness of humanity. I did not have an easy time. I could not work

44

in the shop during the final months, or my relative would have noticed and sent news home. I did not want to ask my mother for money—so I eked out an existence until the baby's birth by selling what little jewellery I had. A week before he was born, my last few crowns were stolen from a cupboard by a washerwoman, so I had to go to the maternity hospital where only very poor women, the outcasts and forgotten, drag themselves in their need. And the child—your child—was born there in the midst of misery. It was a deadly place: strange, everything was strange, we women lying there were strange to each other, lonely and hating one another out of misery, the same torment in that crowded ward full of chloroform and blood, screams and groans. I suffered the humiliation, the mental and physical shame that poverty has to bear from the company of prostitutes and the sick who made our common fate feel terrible, from the cynicism of young doctors who stripped back the sheets from defenceless women with an ironic smile and felt them with false medical expertise, from the greed of the nurses—in there, a woman's bashfulness was crucified with looks and scourged with words. The notice with your name in such a place is all that is left of you, for what lies in the bed is only a twitching piece of flesh felt by the curious, an object to be put on display and studied—the women who bear children at home to husbands waiting affectionately for the birth do not know what it means to give birth to a baby alone and defenceless, as if one were on the laboratory table! If I read the word "hell" in a book to this day, I suddenly and against my conscious will think of that crowded, steamy ward full of sighs, laughter, blood and screams, that slaughterhouse of shame where I suffered.

Forgive me, forgive me for telling you about it. I do so only this one time, never again, never. I have said nothing for eleven years, and I will soon be silent for all eternity; just once I must cry out and say what a high price I paid for my child, the child who was all my bliss and now lies there with no breath left in his body. I had forgotten those hours long ago in his smile and voice, in my happiness, but now he is dead the torment revives, and I had to scream out from my heart just this one time. But I do not accuse you—only God, only God, who made that torment point-less. I do not blame you, I swear it, and never did I rise against you in anger. Even in the hour when I was writhing in labour, when my body burned with shame under the inquisitive eyes of the students, even in the second when the pain tore my soul apart, I never accused you before God. I never regretted those nights or my love for you, I always blessed the day you met me. And if I had to go through the hell of those hours again and knew in advance what was waiting for me I would do it again, my beloved, I would do it again a thousand times over!

Our child died yesterday—you never knew him. Never, even in a fleeting encounter by chance, did your eyes fall on him in passing. I kept myself hidden away from you for a long time once I had my son; my longing for you had become less painful, indeed I think I loved you less passionately, or at least I did not suffer from my love so much now that I had been given the child. I did not want to divide myself between you and him, so I gave myself not to you, a happy man living without me, but to the son who needed me, whom I must nourish, whom I could kiss and embrace. I seemed to be saved from my restless desire for you, saved from my fate by that other self of yours who was really mine—only occasionally, very occasionally, did my feelings humbly send my thoughts out to where you lived. I did just one thing: on your birthday I always sent you a bunch of white roses, exactly the same as the roses you gave me after our first night of love. Have you ever wondered in these ten or eleven years who sent them? Did you perhaps remember the woman to whom you once gave such roses? I don't know, and I will never know your answer. Merely giving them to you out of the dark was enough for me, letting my memory of that moment flower again once a year.

You never knew our poor child—today I blame myself for keeping him from you, because you would have loved him. You never knew the poor boy, never saw him smile when he gently opened his eyelids and cast the clear, happy light of his clever, dark eyes—your eyes!—on me, on the whole world. Oh, he was so cheerful, such a dear; all the light-hearted nature of your being came out again in him in childish form, your quick, lively imagination was reborn. He could play with things for hours, entranced, just as you play with life, and then sit over his books, serious again, his eyebrows raised. He became more and more like you; the duality of gravity and playfulness that is so much your own was visibly beginning to develop in him, and the more like you he grew to be, the more I loved him. He studied hard at school, he could talk French like a little magpie, his exercise books were the neatest in the class, and he was so pretty too, so elegant in his black velvet suit or his white sailor jacket. Wherever he went he was the most elegant of all; when I took him to the Adriatic seaside resort of Grado, women stopped on the beach to stroke his long, fair hair; in Semmering, when he tobogganed downhill, everyone turned admiringly to look at him. He was so good-looking, so tender, so attractive; when he went to be a boarder at the Theresian Academy last year he wore his uniform and his little sword like an eighteenth-century pageboy—now he wears nothing but his nightshirt, poor boy, lying there with pale lips and folded hands.

You may perhaps be wondering how I could afford to bring the child up in such luxury, allowing him to live the cheerful, carefree life of the upper classes. Dearest, I speak to you out of the darkness; I am not ashamed, I will tell you, but do not alarm yourself, beloved—I sold myself. I was not exactly what they call a streetwalker, a common prostitute, but I sold myself. I had rich friends, rich lovers; first I went in search of them, then they sought me out, because I was—did you ever notice?—very beautiful. Everyone to whom I gave myself grew fond of me, they all thanked me and felt attached to me, they all loved me—except for you, except for you, my beloved!

Do you despise me now for telling you that I sold myself?
No, I know you do not; you understand everything, and
you will also understand that I did it only for you, for your
other self, your child. Once, in that ward in the maternity
hospital, I had touched the worst aspect of poverty, I
knew that the poor of this world are always downtrodden,
humiliated, victims, and I would not have your child, your
bright, beautiful son growing up deep down in the scum
of society, in the dark, mean streets, the polluted air of a
room at the back of an apartment building. I did not want
his tender mouth to know the language of the gutter, or
his white body to wear the fusty, shabby garments of the
poor—your child was to have everything, all the riches,
all the ease on earth; he was to rise to be your equal, in
your own sphere of life.

That, my beloved, was my only reason for selling myself.
It was no sacrifice for me, since what people usually call
honour and dishonour meant nothing to me; you did not
love me, and you were the only one to whom my body
truly belonged, so I felt indifferent to anything else that
happened to it. The caresses of those men, even their most
ardent passion did not touch me deeply at all, although
I had to go very carefully with many of them, and my
sympathy for their unrequited love often shook me when
I remembered what my own fate had been. All of them
were good to me, all of them indulged me, they all showed
me respect. There was one in particular, an older man,
a widower who was an imperial count, the same man
who wore himself out going from door to door to get my

49

fatherless child, your child, accepted into the Theresian Academy—he loved me as if I were his daughter. He asked me to marry him three or four times—I could be a countess today, mistress of an enchanting castle in the Tyrol, living a carefree life, because the child would have had a loving father who adored him, and I would have had a quiet, distinguished, kindly husband at my side—but I did not accept him, however often he urged me, and however much my refusals hurt him. Perhaps it was folly, for then I would be living somewhere safe and quiet now, and my beloved child with me, but—why should I not tell you?—I did not want to tie myself down, I wanted to be free for you at any time. In my inmost heart, the depths of my unconscious nature, my old childhood dream that one day you might yet summon me to you, if only for an hour, lived on. And for the possibility of that one hour I rejected all else, so that I would be free to answer your first call. What else had my whole life been since I grew past childhood but waiting, waiting to know your will?

And that hour really did come, but you do not know it. You have no inkling of it, beloved! Even then you did not recognize me—you never, never, never recognized me! I had met you a number of times, at the theatre, at concerts, in the Prater, in the street—every time my heart leapt up, but you looked past me; outwardly I was so different now, the shy child had become a woman, said to be beautiful, wearing expensive clothes, surrounded by admirers: how could you detect in me that shy girl in the dim light of your bedroom? Sometimes the man who was with me greeted you, you greeted him in return and looked at me, but your glance was that of a courteous stranger, appreciative but never recognizing me: strange, terribly strange. Once, I still remember, that failure to recognize me, although I was almost used to it, became a burning torment. I was sitting in a box at the Opera House with a lover and you were in the box next to ours. The lights dimmed during the overture, and I could no longer see your face, I only felt your breath as near to me as it had been that first night, and your hand, your fine and delicate hand lay on the velvet-upholstered partition between our boxes. And at last I was overcome by longing to bend down to that strange but beloved hand, the hand whose touch I had once felt holding me, and kiss it humbly. The music was rising tempestuously around me, my longing was more and more passionate, I had to exert all my self-control and force myself to sit there, so powerfully were my lips drawn to your beloved hand. After the first act I asked my lover to leave with me. I could not bear it any more, knowing that you were sitting beside me in the dark, so strange to me and yet so close.

But the hour did come, it came once more, one last time in my buried, secret life. It was almost exactly a year ago, on the day after your birthday. Strange: I had been thinking of you all those hours, because I always celebrated your birthday like a festival. I had gone out very early in the morning to buy the white roses that I asked the shop to send you, as I did every year, in memory of an hour that you had forgotten. In the afternoon I went out with

51

my son, I took him to Demel's café and in the evening to the theatre; I wanted him, too, to feel from his early youth that this day, although he did not know its significance, was in some mystical fashion an occasion to be celebrated. Then next day I was out with my lover of the time, a rich young manufacturer from Brünn who adored and indulged me, and wanted to marry me like the rest of them—and whose proposals I had turned down apparently for no good reason, as with the rest of them, although he showered presents on me and the child, and was even endearing in his rather awkward, submissive way. We went together to a concert, where we met cheerful companions, had supper in a restaurant in the Ringstrasse, and there, amidst laughter and talking, I suggested going on to the Tabarin, a café with a dance floor. I normally disliked cafés of that kind, with their organized, alcoholic merriment, like all similar kinds of "fun", and usually objected to such suggestions, but this time—as if some unfathomable magical power in me suddenly and unconsciously caused me to suggest it in the midst of the others' cheerful excitement—I had a sudden, inexplicable wish to go, as if something special were waiting for me there. Since I was accustomed to getting my way, they all quickly stood up, we went to the Tabarin, drank champagne, and I fell suddenly into a fit of hectic, almost painful merriment, something unusual in me. I drank and drank, sang sentimental songs with the others, and almost felt an urge to dance or rejoice. But suddenly—I felt as if something either cold or blazing hot had been laid on my heart—I stopped short: you were sitting with some friends at the next table, looking admiringly at me, with an expression of desire, the expression that could always send my entire body into a state of turmoil. For the first time in ten years you were looking at me again with all the unconsciously passionate force of your being. I trembled, and the glass that I had raised almost fell from my hands. Fortunately my companions did not notice my confusion: it was lost in the noise of the laughter and music.

Your gaze was more and more ardent, immersing me entirely in fire. I did not know whether at last, at long last, you had recognized me, or you desired me again as someone else, a stranger. The blood shot into my cheeks, I answered my companions at our table distractedly. You must have noticed how confused your gaze made me. Then, unseen by the others, you signed to me with a movement of your head a request to go out of the café for a moment. You ostentatiously paid your bill, said goodbye to your friends and left, not without first indicating to me again that you would wait for me outside. I was trembling as if in frost, as if in a fever, I could not answer anyone, I could not control my own racing blood. As chance would have it, at that very moment a pair of black dancers launched into one of those newfangled modern dances with clattering heels and shrill cries; everyone was watching them, and I made use of that second. I stood up, told my lover that I would be back in a moment, and followed you.

You were standing outside the cloakroom, waiting for me; your expression brightened as I came out. Smiling, you hurried to meet me; I saw at once that you didn't recognize me, not as the child of the past or the young girl of a couple of years later. Once again you were approaching me as someone new to you, an unknown stranger.

"Would you have an hour to spare for me, too, sometime?" you asked in confidential tones—I sensed, from the assurance of your manner, that you took me for one of those women who can be bought for an evening.

"Yes," I said, the same tremulous yet of course compliant "Yes" that the girl had said to you in the twilit street over a decade ago.

"Then when can we meet?" you asked.

"Whenever you like," I replied—I had no shame in front of you. You looked at me in slight surprise, the same suspiciously curious surprise as you had shown all that time ago when my swift consent had startled you before.

"Could it be now?" you asked, a little hesitantly.

"Yes," I said. "Let's go."

I was going to the cloakroom to collect my coat. Then it occurred to me that my lover had the cloakroom ticket for both our coats. Going back to ask him for it would have been impossible without offering some elaborate reason, but on the other hand I was not going to give up the hour with you that I had longed for all these years. So I did not for a second hesitate; I just threw my shawl over my evening dress and went out into the damp, misty night without a thought for the coat, without a thought for the kindly, affectionate man who had been keeping me, although I was humiliating him in front of his friends, making him look like a fool whose lover runs away from

54

him after years the first time a stranger whistles to her. Oh, I was entirely aware of the vile, shameful ingratitude of my conduct to an honest friend; I felt that I was being ridiculous, and mortally injuring a kind man for ever in my madness—but what was friendship to me, what was my whole life compared with my impatience to feel the touch of your lips again, to hear you speak softly close to me? I loved you so much, and now that it is all over and done with I can tell you so. And I believe that if you summoned me from my deathbed I would suddenly find the strength in myself to get up and go with you.

There was a car outside the entrance, and we drove to your apartment. I heard your voice again, I felt your tender presence close to me, and was as bemused, as childishly happy as before. As I climbed those stairs again after more than ten years—no, no, I cannot describe how I still felt everything doubly in those seconds, the past and the present, and in all of it only you mattered. Not much was different in your room, a few more pictures, more books, and here and there new pieces of furniture, but still it all looked familiar to me. And the vase of roses stood on the desk—my roses, sent to you the day before on your birthday, in memory of someone whom you did not remember, did not recognize even now that she was close to you, hand in hand and lips to lips. But all the same, it did me good to think that you looked after the flowers: it meant that a breath of my love and of myself did touch you.

You took me in your arms. Once again I spent a whole, wonderful night with you. But you did not even recognize my naked body. In bliss, I accepted your expert caresses and saw that your passion draws no distinction between someone you really love and a woman selling herself, that you give yourself up entirely to your desire, unthinkingly squandering the wealth of your nature. You were so gentle and affectionate with me, a woman picked up in the dance café, so warmly and sensitively respectful, yet at the same time enjoying possession of a woman so passionately; once more, dizzy with my old happiness, I felt your unique duality—a knowing, intellectual passion mingled with sensuality. It was what had already brought me under your spell when I was a child. I have never felt such concentration on the moment of the act of love in any other man, such an outburst and reflection of his deepest being—although then, of course, it was to be extinguished in endless, almost inhuman oblivion. But I also forgot myself; who was I, now, in the dark beside you? Was I the ardent child of the past, was I the mother of your child, was I a stranger? Oh, it was all so familiar, I had known it all before, and again it was all so intoxicatingly new on that passionate night. I prayed that it would never end.

But morning came, we got up late, you invited me to stay for breakfast with you. Together we drank the tea that an invisible servant had discreetly placed ready in the dining room, and we talked. Again, you spoke to me with the open, warm confidence of your nature, and again without any indiscreet questions or curiosity about myself. You did not ask my name or where I lived: once more

I was just an adventure to you, an anonymous woman, an hour of heated passion dissolving without trace in the smoke of oblivion. You told me that you were about to go away for some time, you would be in North Africa for two or three months. I trembled in the midst of my happiness, for already words were hammering in my ears: all over, gone and forgotten! I wished I could fall at your feet and cry out, "Take me with you, recognize me at last, at long last, after so many years!" But I was so timid, so cowardly, so slavish and weak in front of you. I could only say, "What a pity!"

You looked at me with a smile. "Are you really sorry?"

Then a sudden wildness caught hold of me. I stood up and looked at you, a long, hard look. And then I said, "The man I loved was always going away too." I looked at you, I looked you right in the eye. Now, now he will recognize me, I thought urgently, trembling.

But you smiled at me and said consolingly, "People come back again."

"Yes," I said, "they come back, but then they have forgotten."

There must have been something odd, something passionate in the way I said that to you. For you rose to your feet as well and looked at me, affectionately and very surprised. You took me by the shoulders. "What's good is not forgotten; I will not forget you," you said, and as you did so you gazed intently at me as if to memorize my image. And as I felt your eyes on me, seeking, sensing, clinging to you with all my being, I thought that at last, at last the

57

spell of blindness would be broken. He will recognize me now, I thought, he will recognize me now! My whole soul trembled in that thought.

But you did not recognize me. No, you did not know me again, and I had never been more of a stranger to you than at that moment, for otherwise—otherwise you could never have done what you did a few minutes later. You kissed me, kissed me passionately again. I had to tidy my hair, which was disarranged, and as I stood looking in the mirror, looking at what it reflected—I thought I would sink to the ground in shame and horror—I saw you discreetly tucking a couple of banknotes of a high denomination in my muff. How I managed not to cry out I do not know, how I managed not to strike you in the face at that moment—you were paying me, who had loved you from childhood, paying me, the mother of your child, for that night! I was a prostitute from the Tabarin to you, nothing more—you had paid me, you had actually paid me! It was not enough for you to forget me, I had to be humiliated as well.

I reached hastily for my things. I wanted to get away, quickly. It hurt too much. I picked up my hat, which was lying on the desk beside the vase of white roses, my roses. Then an irresistible idea came powerfully to my mind: I would make one more attempt to remind you. "Won't you give me one of your white roses?"

"Happily," you said, taking it out of the vase at once.

"But perhaps they were given to you by a woman—a woman who loves you?" I said.

"Perhaps," you said. "I don't know. They were sent to me, and I don't know who sent them; that's why I like them so much."

I looked at you. "Or perhaps they are from a woman you have forgotten."

You seemed surprised. I looked at you hard. Recognize me, my look screamed, recognize me at last! But your eyes returned a friendly, innocent smile. You kissed me once more. But you did not recognize me.

I went quickly to the door, for I could feel tears rising to my eyes, and I did not want you to see them. In the hall—I had run out in such a hurry—I almost collided with your manservant Johann. Diffident and quick to oblige, he moved aside, opened the front door to let me out, and then in that one second—do you hear?—in that one second as I looked at the old man, my eyes streaming with tears, a light suddenly came into his gaze. In that one second—do you hear?—in that one second the old man, who had not seen me since my childhood, knew who I was. I could have knelt to him and kissed his hands in gratitude for his recognition. As it was, I just quickly snatched the banknotes with which you had scourged me out of my muff and gave them to him. He trembled and looked at me in shock—I think he may have guessed more about me at that moment than you did in all your life. All, all the other men had indulged me, had been kind to me—only you, only you forgot me, only you, only you failed to recognize me!

My child is dead, our child—now I have no one left in the world to love but you. But who are you to me, who are you who never, never recognizes me, who passes me by as if I were no more than a stretch of water, stumbling upon me as if I were a stone, you who always goes away, forever leaving me to wait? Once I thought that, volatile as you are, I could keep you in the shape of the child. But he was your child too: overnight he cruelly went away from me on a journey, he has forgotten me and will never come back. I am alone again, more alone than ever, I have nothing, nothing of yours—no child now, not a word, not a line, you have no memory of me, and if someone were to mention my name in front of you, you would hear it as a stranger's. Why should I not wish to die since I am dead to you, why not move on as you moved on from me? No, beloved, I do not blame you, I will not hurl lamentations at you and your cheerful way of life. Do not fear that I shall pester you any more—forgive me, just this once I had to cry out what is in my heart, in this hour when my child lies there dead and abandoned. Just this once I had to speak to you—then I will go back into the darkness in silence again, as I have always been silent to you.

However, you will not hear my cries while I am still alive—only if I am dead will you receive this bequest from me, from one who loved you above all else and whom you never recognized, from one who always waited for you and whom you never summoned. Perhaps, perhaps you will summon me then, and I will fail to keep faith with you for the first time, because when I am dead I will not hear you.

I leave you no picture and no sign, as you left me nothing; you will never recognize me, never. It was my fate in life, let it be my fate in death. I will not call for you in my last hour, I will leave and you will not know my name or my face. I die with an easy mind, since you will not feel it from afar. If my death were going to hurt you, I could not die.

I cannot write any more... my head feels so dulled... my limbs hurt, I am feverish. I think I shall have to lie down. Perhaps it will soon be over, perhaps fate has been kind to me for once, and I shall not have to see them take my child away... I cannot write any more. Goodbye, beloved, goodbye, and thank you... it was good as it was in spite of everything... I will thank you for that until my last breath. I am at ease: I have told you everything, and now you know—or no, you will only guess—how much I loved you, and you will not feel that love is any burden on you. You will not miss me—that consoles me. Nothing in your happy, delightful life will change—I am doing you no harm with my death, and that comforts me, my beloved.

But who... who will always send you white roses on your birthday now? The vase will be empty, the little breath of my life that blew around you once a year will die away as well! Beloved, listen, I beg you... it is the first and last thing I ask you... do it for me every year on your birthday, which is a day when people think of themselves—buy some roses and put them in that vase. Do it, beloved, in the same way as others have a Mass said once a year for someone now dead who was dear to them. I do not believe in God any more, however, and do not want a Mass—I believe only in you, I love only you, and I will live on only in you... oh, only for one day a year, very, very quietly, as I lived near you... I beg you, do that, beloved... it is the first thing that I have ever asked you to do, and the last... thank you... I love you, I love you... goodbye.

His shaking hands put the letter down. Then he thought for a long time. Some kind of confused memory emerged of a neighbour's child, of a young girl, of a woman in the dance café at night, but a vague and uncertain memory, like a stone seen shimmering and shapeless on the bed of a stream of flowing water. Shadows moved back and forth, but he could form no clear picture. He felt memories of emotion, yet did not really remember. It was as if he had dreamt of all these images, dreamt of them often and deeply, but they were only dreams.

Then his eye fell on the blue vase on the desk in front of him. It was empty, empty on his birthday for the first time in years. He shivered; he felt as if a door had suddenly and invisibly sprung open, and cold air from another world was streaming into his peaceful room. He sensed the presence of death, he sensed the presence of undying love: something broke open inside him, and he thought of the invisible woman, incorporeal and passionate, as one might think of distant music.

A STORY TOLD IN TWILIGHT

H AS RAIN BEEN SWEEPING over the city again in the wind? Is that what suddenly makes it so dim in our room? No. The air is silvery clear and still, as it seldom is on these summer days, but it is getting late, and we didn't notice. Only the dormer windows opposite still smile with a faint glow, and the sky above the roof ridge is veiled by golden mist. In an hour's time it will be night. That will be a wonderful hour, for there is no lovelier sight than the slow fading of sunset colour into shadow, to be followed by darkness rising from the ground below, until finally its black tide engulfs the walls, carrying us away into its obscurity. If we sit opposite one another, looking at each other without a word, it will seem, at that hour, as if our familiar faces in the shadows were older and stranger and farther away, as if we had never known them like that, and each of us was now seeing the other across a wide space and over many years. But you say you don't want silence now, because in silence one hears, apprehensively, the clock breaking time into a hundred tiny splinters, and our breathing will sound as loud as the breathing of a sick man. You want me to tell you a story. Willingly. But not about me, for our life in these big cities is short of experience, or so it seems to us, because we do not yet know what is really our own in them. However, I will tell you a story fit for this hour that really loves only silence, and I would wish it to have something about it of the warm, soft, flowing twilight now hovering mistily outside our windows.

I don't remember just how I came to know this story. All I do know is that I was sitting here for a long time early this afternoon, reading a book, then putting it down again, drowsing in my dreams, perhaps sleeping lightly. And suddenly I saw figures stealing past the walls, and I could hear what they were saying and look into their lives. But when I wanted to watch them moving away, I found myself awake again and on my own. The book lay at my feet. When I picked it up to look for those characters in it, I couldn't find the story any more; it was as if it had fallen out of the pages into my hands, or as if it had never been there at all. Perhaps I had dreamt it, or seen it in one of those bright clouds that came to our city today from distant lands, to carry away the rain that has been depressing us for so long. Did I hear it in the artless old song that an organ-grinder was playing with a melancholy creaking sound under my window, or had someone told it to me years ago? I don't know. Such stories often come into my mind, and I let them take their playful course, running through my fingers, which I allow to drop them as you might caress ears of wheat and long-stemmed flowers in passing without picking them. All I do is dream them, beginning with a sudden brightly coloured image and moving towards a gentler end, but I do not hold and keep them. However, you want me to tell you a story today, so I will tell it to you now, when twilight fills us with a longing to see some bright, lively thing before our eyes, starved as they are in this grey light.

How shall I begin? I feel I must pluck a moment out of the darkness, an image and a character, because that is how those strange dreams of mine begin. Yes, now I remember. I see a slender youth walking down a broad flight of steps leading out of a castle. It is night, and a night of dim moonlight, but I see the whole outline of his supple body, and his features stand out clearly. He is remarkably good-looking. His black hair falls smoothly over his high—almost too high—forehead, combed in a childish style, and his hands, reaching out before him in the dark to feel the warmth of the air after a sunlit day, are delicate and finely formed. His footsteps are hesitant. Dreamily, he climbs down to the large garden, where the rounded treetops rustle; the white path of a single broad avenue leads through it.

I don't know when all this is set, whether yesterday or fifty years ago, and I don't know where; but I think it must be in England or Scotland, the only places where I am sure there are such tall, massive stone castles. From a distance they look menacing, like fortresses, and reveal their bright gardens full of flowers only to an eye familiar with them. Yes, now I know for certain: it is to the north, in Scotland. Only there are the summer nights so light that the sky has a milky, opalescent glow, and the fields are never entirely

67

dark, so that everything seems full of a soft radiance, and only the shadows drop, like huge black birds, down to pale expanses of countryside. Yes, it's in Scotland, I remember that now for certain; and if I racked my brain I would also find the names of this baronial castle and the boy, because now the darkness around my dream is beginning to peel away, and I feel it all as distinctly as if it were not memory but experience. The boy has come to spend the summer with his married sister, and in the hospitable way of distinguished British families he finds that he is not alone; in the evening there is a whole party of gentlemen who have come for the field sports of shooting and fishing, and their wives, with a few young girls, tall, handsome people, who in their cheerfulness and youth play laughing, but not noisily, to the sound of the echo from the ancient walls. By day they ride horses, there are dogs about, two or three boats glitter on the river, and liveliness without frantic activity helps the day to pass quickly and pleasantly.

But it is evening now, the company around the dinner table has broken up. The gentlemen are sitting in the great hall, smoking and playing cards; until midnight, white light, quivering at the edges, spills out of the bright windows into the park, sometimes accompanied by a full-throated, jocular roar of laughter. Most of the ladies have already gone to their rooms, although a few of them may still be talking to each other in the entrance hall of the castle. So the boy is on his own in the evening. He is not allowed to join the gentlemen yet, or only briefly, and he feels shy in the presence of ladies because when he opens a door

68

they suddenly lower their voices, and he senses that they are discussing matters he isn't meant to hear. And he doesn't like their company anyway, because they ask him questions as if he were still a child, and only half-listen to his answers; they make use of him to do them all sorts of small favours, and then thank him in the tone they would use with a good little boy. He thought he would go to bed, but his room was too hot, full of still, sultry air. They had forgotten to close the windows during the day, so the sun had made itself at home in here, almost setting light to the table, leaving the bedstead hot to the touch, clinging heavily to the walls, and its warm breath still comes out of the corners and from behind curtains. And moreover it was still so early—and outside, the summer night shone like a white candle, peaceful, with no wind, as motionless as if it longed for nothing. So the boy goes down the tall castle steps again and towards the garden, which is rimmed by the dark sky like a saint's halo. Here the rich fragrance given off by many invisible flowers comes enticingly to meet him. He feels strange. In all the confused sensations of his fifteen years of life, he couldn't have said exactly why, but his lips are quivering as if he has to say something in the night air, or must raise his hands and close his eyes for a long time. He seems to have some mysterious familiarity with this summer night, now at rest, something that calls for words or a gesture of greeting.

Then, all of a sudden, as he goes deeper into the darkness, an extraordinary thing happens. The gravel behind him crunches slightly, and as he turns, startled, all he sees

is a tall white form, bright and fluttering, coming towards
him, and in astonishment he feels strong and yet caught,
without any violence, in a woman's embrace. A soft, warm
body presses close to his, a trembling hand quickly caresses
his hair and bends his head back; reeling, he feels a stranger's open mouth like a fruit against his own, quivering lips
fastening on his. The face is so close to him that he cannot
see its features. And he dares not look, because shudders
are running through his body like pain, so that he has to
close his eyes and give himself up to those burning lips
without any will of his own; he is their prey. Hesitantly,
uncertainly, as if asking a question, his arms now go round
the stranger's body, and, suddenly intoxicated, he holds it
close to his own. Avidly, his hands move over its soft outline,
fall still and then tremble as they move on again more and
more feverishly, carried away. And now the whole weight of
her body, pressing ever more urgently against him, bending forward, a delightful burden, rests on his own yielding
breast. He feels as if he were sinking and flowing away
under her fast-breathing urgency, and is already weak at
the knees. He thinks of nothing, he does not wonder how
this woman came to him, or what her name is, he merely
drinks in the desire of those strange, moist lips with his
eyes closed, until he is intoxicated by them, drifting away
with no will or mind of his own on a vast tide of passion.
He feels as if stars had suddenly fallen to earth, there is
such a shimmering before his eyes, everything flickers in
the air like sparks, burning whatever he touches. He does
not know how long all this lasts, whether he has been held

in this soft chain for hours or seconds; in this wild, sensual struggle he feels that everything is blazing up and drifting away, he is staggering in a wonderful kind of vertigo.

Then suddenly, with an abrupt movement, the chain of heat holding them breaks. Brusquely, almost angrily, the woman loosens the embrace that held him so close; she stands erect, and already a shaft of white light is running past the trees, clear and fast, and has gone before he can raise his hands to seize it and stop her.

Who was she? And how long had it lasted? Dazed, with a sense of oppressive uneasiness, he stands up, propping himself against a tree. Slowly, cool thought returns to the space between his fevered temples: his life suddenly seems to him to have moved forward a thousand hours. Could his confused dreams of women and passion suddenly have come true? Or was it only a dream? He feels himself, touches his hair. Yes, it is damp at his hammering temples, damp and cool from the dew on the grass into which they had fallen. Now it all flashes before his mind's eye again, he feels those burning lips once more, breathes in the strange, exciting, sensual perfume clinging to her dress, tries to remember every word she spoke—but none of them come back to him.

And now, with a sudden shock of alarm, he remembers that in fact she said nothing at all, not even his name; that he heard only her sighs spilling over and her convulsively restrained sobs of desire threatening to break out, that he knows the fragrance of her tousled hair, the hot pressure of her breasts, the smooth enamel of her skin, he knows

71

STEFAN ZWEIG

that her figure, her breath, all her quivering feelings were his—and yet he has no idea of the identity of this woman who has overwhelmed him with her love in the dark. He knows that he must now try to find a name to give to his happy astonishment.

And then the extraordinary experience that he has just shared with a woman seems to him a poor thing, very petty compared to the sparkling mystery staring at him out of the dark with alluring eyes. Who was she? He swiftly reviews all the possible candidates, assembling in his mind's eye the images of all the women staying here at the castle; he recalls every strange hour, excavates from his memory every conversation he has had with them, every smile of the only five or six women who could be part of this puzzle. Young Countess E., perhaps, who so often quarrelled violently with her ageing husband, or his uncle's young wife, who had such curiously gentle yet iridescent eyes, or—and he was startled by this idea—one of the three sisters, his cousins, who are so like each other in their proud, haughty, abrupt manner. No—these were all cool, circumspect people. In recent years he had often felt sick, or an outcast, when secret stirrings in him began disturbing and flickering in his dreams. He had envied all who were, or seemed to be, so calm, so well-balanced and lacking in desires, had been afraid of his awakening passion as if it were an infirmity. And now?... But who, which of them all could be so deceptive?

Slowly, that insistent question drives the frenzy out of his blood. It is late now, the lights in the hall where guests were playing cards are out, he is the only guest in the castle still awake, he—and perhaps also that unknown woman. Slowly, weariness comes over him. Why go on thinking about it? A glance, a spark glimpsed between someone's eyelids, the secret pressure of his hand must surely tell him everything tomorrow. Dreamily, he climbs the steps, as dreamily as he climbed down them, but he feels so very different now. His blood is still slightly agitated, but the warm room seems to him clearer and cooler than it was.

When he wakes next morning, the horses down outside the castle are already stamping and scraping their hooves on the ground; he hears voices, laughter, and his name is called now and then. He quickly leaps out of bed—he has missed breakfast—dresses at high speed and runs downstairs, where the rest of the party cheerfully wish him a good morning. "What a late riser you are!" laughs Countess E., and there is laughter in her clear eyes as well. His avid look falls on her face; no, it couldn't be the Countess, her laughter is too carefree. "I hope you had sweet dreams," the young woman teases him, but her delicate build seems to him too slight for his companion last night. With a question in his eyes, he looks from face to face, but sees no smiling reflection answering it on any of them.

They ride out into the country. He assesses each voice, his eyes dwell on every line and undulation of the women's bodies as they move on horseback, he observes the way they bend, the way they raise their arms. At the luncheon table he leans close to them in conversation, to catch the scent of their lips or the sultry warmth of their hair, but nothing, nothing gives him any sign, not a fleeting trail for his heated thoughts to pursue. The day draws out endlessly towards evening. If he tries to read a book, the lines run over the edge of the pages and suddenly lead out into the garden, and it is night again, that strange night, and he feels the unknown woman's arms embracing him once more. Then he drops the book from his trembling hands and decides to go down to the little pool. But suddenly, surprised by himself, he finds that he is standing on that very spot again. He feels feverish at dinner that evening, his hands are distracted, moving restlessly back and forth as if pursued, his eyes retreat shyly under their lids. Not until the others—at last, at last!—push back their chairs is he happy, and soon he is running out of his room and into the park, up and down the white path that seems to shimmer like milky mist beneath his feet, going up and down it, up and down hundreds, thousands of times. Are the lights on in the great hall yet? Yes, they come on at last, and at last there is light in a few of the first-floor windows. The ladies have gone upstairs. Now, if she is going to come, it can be only a matter of minutes; but every minute stretches to breaking point, fuming with impatience. Up and down the path, up and down, he is moving convulsively back and forth as if worked by invisible wires.

And then, suddenly, the white figure comes hurrying down the steps, fast, much too fast for him to recognize her. She seems to be made of glinting moonlight, or a lost, drifting wisp of mist among the trees, chased this way by the wind and now, now in his arms. They close firmly as a claw around that wild body, heated and throbbing from her fast running. It is the same as yesterday, a single moment with this warm wave beating against his breast, and he thinks he will faint with the sweet throbbing of her heart and flow away in a stream of dark desire. But then the frenzy abruptly dies down, and he holds back his fiery feelings. He must not lose himself in that wonderful pleasure, give himself up to those lips fixed on his, before he knows what name to give this body pressed so close that it is as if her heart were beating loudly in his own chest! He bends his head back from her kiss to see her face, but shadows are falling, mingling with her hair; the twilight makes it look dark. The tangled trees grow too close together, and the light of the moon, veiled in cloud, is not strong enough for him to make out her features. He sees only her eyes shining, glowing stones sprinkled deep down somewhere, set in faintly gleaming marble.

Now he wants to hear a word, just one splinter of her voice breaking away. "Who are you?" he demands. "Tell me who you are!" But that soft, moist mouth offers only kisses, no words. He tries to force a word out of her, a cry of pain, he squeezes her arm, digs his nails into its flesh; but he is aware only of his own gasping, heated breath, and of the sultry heat of her obstinately silent lips that only moan a little now and then—whether in pain or pleasure he does not know. And it sends him nearly mad to realize that he has no power over this defiant will, that this woman coming out of the dark takes him without giving herself

away to him, that he has unbounded power over her body
and its desires, yet cannot command her name. Anger rises
in him and he fends off her embrace; but she, feeling his
arms slacken and aware of his uneasiness, caresses his hair
soothingly, enticingly with her excited hand. And then, as
her fingers move, he feels something make a slight ringing
sound against his forehead, something metal, a medallion
or coin that hangs loose from her bracelet. An idea suddenly occurs to him. As if in the transports of passion, he
presses her hand to him, and in so doing embeds the coin
deep in his half-bared arm until he feels its surface digging
into his skin. He is sure of having a sign to follow now, and
with it burning against him he willingly gives himself up
to the passion he has held back. Now he presses deep into
her body, sucks the desire from her lips, falling into the
mysteriously pleasurable ardour of a wordless embrace.

And then, when she suddenly jumps up and takes flight,
just as she did yesterday, he does not try to hold her back,
for he is already feverish with curiosity to see the sign.
He runs to his room, turns up the dim lamplight until it
is bright, and bends avidly over the mark left by the coin
in his arm.

It is no longer entirely clear, the full outline is indistinct;
but one corner is still engraved red and sharp on his flesh,
unmistakably precise. There are angular corners; the coin
must have eight sides, medium-sized like a penny but with
more of a raised surface, because the impression here
is still deep, corresponding to the height of the surface.
The mark burns like fire as he examines it so greedily; it

suddenly hurts him, like a wound, and only now that he dips his hand in cold water does the painful burning go away. So the medallion is octagonal; he feels certain of that now. Triumph sparkles in his eyes. Tomorrow he will know everything.

Next morning he is one of the first down at the breakfast table. The only ladies present are an elderly old maid, his sister and Countess E. They are all in a cheerful mood, and their lively conversation passes him by. He has all the more opportunity for his observations. His glance swiftly falls on the Countess's slim wrist; she is not wearing a bracelet. He can speak to her without agitation now, but his eyes keep going nervously to the door. Then his cousins, the three sisters, come in together. Uneasiness stirs in him again. He catches a glimpse of the jewellery they wear pushed up under their sleeves, but they sit down too quickly for a good view: Kitty with her chestnut-brown hair opposite him; blonde Margot; and Elisabeth, whose hair is so fair that it shines like silver in the dark and flows golden in the sun. All three, as usual, are cool, quiet and reserved, stiff with the dignity he dislikes so much about them; after all, they are not much older than he is, and were his playmates for years. His uncle's young wife has not come down yet. The boy's heart is more and more restless now that he feels the moment of revelation is so close, and suddenly he decides that he almost likes the mysterious torment of secrecy. However, his eyes are full of curiosity; they move around the edge of the table, where the women's hands lie at rest on the white cloth or wander slowly like ships in

77

a bright bay. He sees only their hands, and they suddenly seem to him like creatures with a life and soul of their own, characters on a stage. Why is the blood throbbing at his temples like that? All three cousins, he sees in alarm, are wearing bracelets, and the idea that it could be one of these three proud and outwardly immaculate young women, whom he has never known, even in childhood, as anything but unapproachable and reserved, confuses him. Which of them could it be? Kitty, whom he knows least because she is the eldest, Margot with her abrupt manner, or little Elisabeth? He dares not wish it to be any of them. Secretly, he wants it to be none of them, or he wants not to know. But now his desire carries him away.

"Could I ask you to pour me another cup of tea, please, Kitty?" His voice sounds as if he has sand in his throat. He passes her his cup; now she must raise her arm and reach over the table to him. Now—he sees a medallion dangling from her bracelet and for a moment his hand stops dead, but no, it is a green stone in a round setting that clinks softly against the porcelain. His glance gratefully rests on Kitty's brown hair.

It takes him a moment to get his breath back.

"May I trouble you for a lump of sugar, Margot?" A slender hand comes to life on the table, stretches, picks up a silver bowl and passes it over. And there—his hand shakes slightly—he sees, where the wrist disappears into her sleeve, an old silver coin dangling from a flexible bracelet. The coin has eight sides, is the size of a penny and is obviously a family heirloom of some kind. But octagonal, with the sharp corners that dug into his flesh yesterday. His hand is no steadier, and he misses his aim with the sugar tongs at first; only then does he drop a lump of sugar into his tea, which he forgets to drink.

Margot! The name is burning on his lips in a cry of the utmost surprise, but he clenches his teeth and bites it back. He hears her speaking now—and her voice sounds to him as strange as if someone were speaking from a stand at a show—cool, composed, slightly humorous, and her breath is so calm that he almost takes fright at the thought of the terrible lie she is living. Is this really the same woman whose unsteady breath he soothed yesterday, from whose moist lips he drank kisses, who falls on him by night like a beast of prey? Again and again he stares at those lips. Yes, the pride, the reserve, could be taking refuge there and nowhere else, but what is there to show the fire within her?

He looks harder at her face, as if seeing it for the first time. And for the first time he really feels, rejoicing, trembling with happiness and almost near tears, how beautiful she is in her pride, how enticing in her secrecy. His gaze traces, with delight, the curving line of her eyebrows suddenly rising to a sharp angle, looks deep into the cool, gemstone hue of her grey-green eyes, kisses the pale, slightly translucent skin of her cheeks, imagines her lips, now sharply tensed, curving more softly for a kiss, wanders around her pale hair, and, quickly moving down again, takes in her whole figure with delight. He has never known her until this moment. Now he rises from the table and finds that his knees are trembling. He is drunk with looking at her as if on strong wine.

Then his sister calls down below. The horses are ready for the morning ride, prancing nervously, impatiently champing at the bit. One guest after another mounts, and then they ride in a bright cavalcade down the broad avenue through the garden. First at a slow trot, with a sedate harmony that is out of tune with the racing rhythm of the boy's blood. But then, beyond the gate, they give the horses their heads, storming down the road and into the meadows to left and right, where a slight morning mist still lingers. There must have been a heavy fall of dew overnight, for under the veil of mist, trembling dewdrops glitter like sparks, and the air is deliciously cool, as if chilled by a waterfall somewhere near. The close-packed group soon strings out, the chain breaks into colourful separate links and a few riders have already disappeared into the woods among the hills.

Margot is one of the riders in the lead. She loves the wild exhilaration, the passionate tug of the wind at her hair, the indescribable sense of pressing forward at a fast gallop. The boy is storming on behind her; he sees her proud body sitting very erect, tracing a beautiful line in her swift movement. He sometimes sees her slightly flushed face, the light in her eyes, and now that she is living out her own strength with such passion he knows her again. Desperately, he feels his love and longing flare vehemently up. He is overcome by an impetuous wish to take hold of her all of a sudden, sweep her off her horse and into his arms, to drink from those ravenous lips again, to feel the

shattering throb of her agitated heart against his breast.
He strikes his horse's flank, and it leaps forward with a
whinny. Now he is beside her, his knee almost touching
hers, their stirrups clink slightly together. He must say it
now, he must.

"Margot," he stammers.

She turns her head, her arched brows shoot up. "Yes,
what is it, Bob?" Her tone of voice is perfectly cool. And
her eyes are cool as well, showing no emotion.

A shiver runs all the way down him to his knees. What
had he been going to say? He can't remember. He stammers something about turning back.

"Are you tired?" she says, with what sounds to him like
a touch of sarcasm.

"No, but the others are so far behind," he manages to
say. Another moment, he feels, and he will be impelled
to do something senseless—reach his arms out to her, or
begin shedding tears, or strike out at her with the riding
crop that is shaking in his hand as if it were electrically
charged. Abruptly he pulls his horse back, making it
rear for a moment. She races on ahead, erect, proud,
unapproachable.

The others soon catch up with him. There is a lively
conversation in progress to both sides of him, but the words
and laughter pass him by, making no sense, like the hard
clatter of the horses' hooves. He is tormenting himself for
his failure to summon up the courage to tell her about his
love and force her to confess hers, and his desire to tame
her grows wilder and wilder, veiling his eyes like a red mist

above the land before him. Why didn't he answer scorn with scorn? Unconsciously he urges his horse on, and now the heat of his speed eases his mind. Then the others call out that it is time to turn back. The sun has crept above the hills and is high in the midday sky. A soft, smoky fragrance wafts from the fields, colours are bright now and burn the eyes like molten gold. Sultry, heavy heat billows out over the land, the sweating horses are trotting more drowsily, with warm steam rising from them, breathing hard. Slowly the procession forms again, cheerfulness is more muted than before, conversation more desultory.

Margot too is in sight again. Her horse is foaming at the mouth, white specks of foam cling trembling to her riding habit, and the round bun into which she has pinned up her hair threatens to come undone, held in place only loosely by its clasps. The boy stares as if enchanted at the tangle of blonde hair, and the idea that it might suddenly all come down, flowing in wild tresses, maddens him with excitement. Already the arched garden gate at the end of the avenue is in sight, and beyond it the broad avenue up to the castle. Carefully, he guides his horse past the others, is the first to arrive, jumps down, hands the reins to a groom and waits for the cavalcade. Margot comes last. She trots up very slowly, her body relaxed, leaning back, exhausted as if by pleasure. She must look like that, he senses, when she has blunted the edge of her frenzy, she must have looked like that yesterday and the evening before. The memory makes him impetuous again. He goes over to her and, breathlessly, helps her down from the horse.

As he is holding the stirrup, his hand feverishly clasps her slender ankle. "Margot," he groans, murmuring her name softly. She does not so much as look at him in answer, taking the hand he is holding out casually as she gets down.

"Margot, you're so wonderful," he stammers again.

She gives him a sharp look, her eyebrows rising steeply again. "I think you must be drunk, Bob! What on earth are you talking about?"

But angry with her for pretending, blind with passion, he presses the hand that he is still holding firmly to himself as if to plunge it into his breast. At that, Margot, flushing angrily, gives him such a vigorous push that he sways, and she walks rapidly past him. All this has happened so fast and so abruptly that no one has noticed, and now it seems to him, too, like nothing but an alarming dream.

He is so pale and distracted all the rest of the day that the blonde Countess strokes his hair in passing and asks if he is all right. He is so angry that when his dog jumps up at him, barking, he chases it away with a kick; he is so clumsy in playing games that the girls laugh at him. The idea that now she will not come this evening poisons his blood, makes him bad-tempered and surly. They all sit out in the garden together at teatime, Margot opposite him, but she does not look at him. Magnetically attracted, his eyes keep tentatively glancing at hers, which are cool as grey stone, returning no echo. It embitters him to think that she is playing with him like this. Now, as she turns brusquely away from him, he clenches his fist and feels he could easily knock her down.

"What's the matter, Bob? You look so pale," says a voice suddenly. It is little Elisabeth, Margot's sister. There is a soft, warm light in her eyes, but he does not notice it. He feels rather as if he were caught in some disreputable act, and says angrily, "Leave me alone, will you? You and your damned concern for me!" Then he regrets it, because the colour drains out of Elisabeth's own face, she turns away and says, with a hint of tears in her voice, "How oddly you're behaving today." Everyone is looking at him with disapproval, almost menacingly, and he himself feels that he is in the wrong. But then, before he can apologize, a hard voice, bright and sharp as the blade of a knife, Margot's voice, speaks across the table. "If you ask me, Bob is behaving very badly for his age. We're wrong to treat him as a gentleman or even an adult." This from Margot, Margot who gave him her lips only last night! He feels everything going round in circles, there is a mist before his eyes. Rage seizes him. "You of all people should know!" he says in an unpleasant tone of voice, and gets up from the table. His movement was so abrupt that his chair falls over behind him, but he does not turn back.

And yet, senseless as it seems even to him, that evening he is down in the garden again, praying to God that she may come. Perhaps all that had been nothing but pretence and waywardness—no, he wouldn't ask her any more questions or be angry with her, if only she would come, if only he could feel once again the bitter desire of those soft, moist lips against his mouth, sealing all its questions. The hours seem to have gone to sleep; night, an apathetic, limp animal, lies in front of the castle; time drags out to an insane length. The faintly buzzing grass around him seems to be animated by mocking voices; the twigs and branches gently moving, playing with their shadows and the faint glow of evening light, are like mocking hands. All sounds are confused and strange, they irritate him more painfully than silence. Once a dog begins barking out in the countryside, and once a shooting star crosses the sky and falls somewhere behind the castle. The night seems brighter and brighter, the shadows of the trees above the garden path darker and darker, and those soft sounds are more and more confused. Drifting clouds envelop the sky in sombre, melancholy darkness. This loneliness falls on his burning heart.

The boy walks up and down, more and more vigorously, faster and faster. Sometimes he angrily strikes a tree, or rubs a piece of its bark in his fingers, rubbing so furiously that they bleed. No, she is not going to come, he knew it all along, but he doesn't want to believe it because then she will never come again, never. It is the bitterest moment of his life. And he is still so youthfully passionate that he flings himself down hard in the damp moss, digging his hands into the earth, tears on his cheeks, sobbing softly and bitterly as he never wept as a child, and as he will never be able to weep again.

Then a faint cracking sound in the undergrowth suddenly rouses him from his despair. And as he leaps up, blindly holding out his searching hands, he finds that he is holding—and how wonderful is its sudden, warm impact on his breast—he is holding the body of which he dreamt so wildly in his arms again. A sob breaks from his throat, his whole being is dissolved in a vast convulsion, and he holds her tall, curving body so masterfully to his that a moan comes from those strange, silent lips. As he feels her groan, held in his power, he knows for the first time that he has mastered her and is not, as he was yesterday and the day before, the prey of her moods; a desire overcomes him to torment her for the torment he has felt for what seems like a hundred hours, to chastise her for her defiance, for those scornful words this evening in front of the others, for the mendacious game she is playing. Hatred is so inextricably intertwined with his burning desire that their embrace is more of a battle than a loving encounter. He catches hold of her slim wrists so that her whole breathless body writhes, trembling, and then holds her so stormily against him again that she cannot move, only groan quietly again and again, whether in pleasure or pain he does not know. But he cannot get a word out of her. Now, when he forces his lips on hers, sucking at them to stifle that faint moaning, he feels something warm and wet on them, blood, blood running where her teeth have bitten so hard into his lips. And so he torments her until he suddenly feels his strength flagging, and the hot wave of desire rises in him, and now they are both gasping, breast to breast. Flames have fallen overnight, stars seem to flicker in front of his eyes, everything is crazy, his thoughts circle more wildly, and all of it has only one name: Margot. Muted, but from the depths of his heart, he finally, in a burning torrent, gets out her name in mingled rejoicing and despair, expressing longing, hatred, anger and love at the same time. It comes out in a single cry filled with his three days of torment: Margot, Margot. And to his ears, all the music in the world lies in those two syllables.

A shock passes through his body. All at once the fervour of their embrace dies down, a brief, wild thrust, a sob, weeping comes from her throat, and again there is fire in her movements, but only to tear herself away as if from a touch she hates. Surprised, he tries to hold her, but she struggles with him; as she bends her face close he feels tears of anger running down her cheeks, and her slender body writhes like a snake. Suddenly, with an embittered movement of violence, she throws him off and runs. Her white dress shows among the trees, and is then drowned in darkness.

So there he stands, alone again, shocked and confused as he was the first time, when warmth and passion suddenly fell into his arms. The stars gleam with moisture before his eyes, and his blood thrusts sharp sparks into his brow from within. What has happened? He makes his way through the row of trees, growing less densely here, and farther into the garden, where he knows the little fountain will be playing. He lets its water soothe his hand, white, silvery water that murmurs softly to him and shines beautifully in the reflection of the moon as it slowly emerges from the clouds again. And then, now that he sees more clearly, wild grief comes over him as if the mild wind had blown it down out of the trees. His warm tears rise, and now he feels, more strongly and clearly than in those moments of their convulsive embrace, how much he loves Margot. Everything that went before has fallen away from him, the shuddering frenzy of possession, his anger at her withholding of her secret; love in all its fullness, sweetly melancholy, surrounds him, a love almost without longing; but it is overpowering.

Why did he torment her like that? Hasn't she shown him incredible generosity on these three nights, hasn't his life suddenly emerged from a gloomy twilight into a sparkling, dangerously bright light since she taught him tenderness and the wild ardour of love? And then she left him, in tears of anger! A soft, irresistible wish for reconciliation wells up in him, for a mild, calm word, a wish to hold her quiet in his arms, asking nothing, and tell her how grateful he is to her. Yes, he will go to her in all humility and tell her how purely he loves her, saying he will never mention her name again or force an answer out of her that she does not want to give.

The silvery water flows softly, and he thinks of her tears. Perhaps she is all alone in her room now, he thinks, with only this whispering night to listen to her, a night that listens to all and consoles no one. This night when he is both far from her and near her, without seeing a glimmer of her hair, hearing a word in her voice half lost on the wind, and yet he is caught inextricably, his soul in hers—this night becomes unbearable agony to him. And his longing to be near her, even lying outside her door like a dog or standing as a beggar below her window, is irresistible.

As he hesitantly steals out of the darkness of the trees, he sees that there is still light in her window on the first floor. It is a faint light; its yellow shimmering scarcely even illuminates the leaves of the spreading sycamore tree that is trying to knock on the window with its branches as if they were hands, stretching them out, then withdrawing them again in the gentle breeze, a dark, gigantic eavesdropper outside the small, shining pane. The idea that Margot is awake behind the shining glass, perhaps still shedding tears or thinking about him, upsets the boy so much that he has to lean against the tree to keep himself from swaying.

He stares up as if spellbound. The white curtains waft restlessly out, playing in the light wind, seeming now deep gold in the radiance of the warm lamplight, now silvery when they blow forward into the shaft of moonlight that seeps, flickering, through the leaves. And the window, opening inward, mirrors the play of light and shade as a loosely strung tissue of light reflections. But to the fevered boy now staring up out of the shadows, hot-eyed, dark runes telling a tale seem to be written there on a blank surface. The flowing shadows, the silvery gleam that passes over that black surface like faint smoke—these fleeting perceptions fill his imagination with trembling images. He sees Margot, tall and beautiful, her hair—oh, that wild, blonde hair—flowing loose, his own restlessness in her blood, pacing up and down her room, sees her feverish in her sultry passion, sobbing with rage. As if through glass, he now sees, through the high walls, the smallest of her movements when she raises her hands or sinks into an armchair, and her silent, desperate staring at the starlit sky. He even thinks, when the pane lights up for a moment, that he sees her face anxiously bend to look down into the slumbering garden, looking for him. And then his wild emotion gets the better of him; keeping his voice low, and yet urgent, he calls up her name: Margot! Margot!

Wasn't that something scurrying over the blank surface like a veil, white and fast? He thinks he saw it clearly. He strains his ears, but nothing is moving. The soft breath of the drowsy trees and the silken whispering in the grass swell, carried on the gentle wind, now farther away, now louder again, a warm wave gently dying down. The night is peaceful, the window is silent, a silver frame round a darkened picture. Didn't she hear him? Or doesn't she want to hear him any more? That trembling glow around the window confuses him. His heart beats hard, expressing the longing in his breast, beats against the bark of the tree, and the bark itself seems to tremble at such passion. All he knows is that he must see her now, must speak to her now, even if he were to call her name so loud that people came to see what was going on, and others woke from sleep. He feels that something must happen at this point, the most senseless of ideas seems to him desirable, just as everything is easily achieved in a dream. Now that his glance moves up to the window again, he suddenly sees the tree leaning against it reach out a branch like a signpost, and his hand clings harder to its trunk. Suddenly it is all clear to him: he must climb up there—the trunk is broad, but feels soft and silken—and once up the tree he will call to her just outside her window. Close to her up there, he will talk to her, and he won't come down again until she has forgiven him. He does not stop to think for a second, he sees only the window, enticing him, gleaming faintly, and feels that the tree is on his side, sturdy and broad enough to take his weight. With a couple of quick movements he swings himself up, and already his hands are holding a branch. He energetically hauls his body after them, and now he is high in the tree, almost at the top of the leaf canopy swaying beneath him as it might do in alarm. The rustling sound of the leaves ripples on to the last of them, and the branch bends closer to the window as if to warn the unsuspecting girl. Now the boy, as he climbs, can see the white ceiling of her room, and in the middle of it, sparkling gold, the circle of light cast by the lamp. And he knows, trembling slightly with excitement, that in a moment he will see Margot herself, weeping or still sobbing or in the naked desire of her body. His arms slacken, but he catches himself again. Slowly, he makes his way along the branch turned to her window; his knees are bleeding a little, there is a cut on his hand, but he climbs on, and is now almost within the light from the window. A broad tangle of leaves still conceals the view, the final scene he longs so much to see, and the ray of light is already falling on him as he bends forward, trembling—and his body rocks, he loses his balance and falls tumbling to the ground.

He hits the grass with a soft, hollow impact, like a heavy fruit falling. Up in the castle, a figure leans out of the window, looking around uneasily, but nothing moves in the darkness, which is still as a millpond that has swallowed up a drowning man. Soon the light at the window goes out and the garden is left to itself again, in the uncertain twilight gleam above the silent shadows.

After a few minutes the fallen figure wakes to consciousness. His eyes stare up for a second to where a pale sky with a few wandering stars in it looks coldly down on him. But then he feels a sudden piercing, agonizing pain in his right foot, a pain that almost makes him scream at the first movement he attempts. Suddenly he knows what has happened to him. He also knows that he can't stay lying here under Margot's window, he can't call for help to anyone, must not raise his voice or make much noise as he moves. Blood is running from his forehead; he must have hit a stone or a piece of wood on the turf, but he wipes it away with his hand to keep it from running into his eyes. Then, curled on his left side, he tries slowly working his way forward by ramming his hands into the earth. Every time something touches or merely jars his broken leg, pain flares up, and he is afraid of losing consciousness again. But he drags himself slowly on. It takes him almost half an hour to reach the steps, and his arms already feel weak. Cold sweat mingles on his brow with the sticky blood still oozing out. The last and worst of it is still to come: he must get to the top of the steps, and he works his way very slowly up them, in agony. When he is right at the top, reaching for the balustrade, his breath rattles in his throat. He drags himself a little farther, to the door into the room where the gentlemen play cards, and where he can hear voices and see a light. He hauls himself up by the handle, and suddenly, as if flung in, he falls into the brightly lit room as the door gives way.

He must present a gruesome sight, stumbling in like that, blood all over his face, smeared with garden soil, and then falling to the floor like a clod of earth, because the gentlemen spring up wildly. Chairs fall over backwards with a clatter, they all hurry to help him. He is carefully laid on the sofa. He just manages to babble something about tumbling down the steps on his way to go for a walk in the park, and then it is as if black ribbons fall on his eyes, waver back and forth, and surround him entirely. He falls into a faint, and knows no more.

A horse is saddled, and someone rides to the nearest town to fetch a doctor. The castle, startled into wakefulness, is full of ghostly activity: lights tremble like glow-worms in the corridors, voices whisper, asking what has happened from their bedroom doors, the servants timidly appear, drowsy with sleep, and finally the unconscious boy is carried up to his room.

The doctor ascertains that he has indeed broken his leg, and reassures everyone by telling them that there is no danger. However, the victim of the accident will have to lie motionless with his leg bound up for a long time. When the boy is told, he smiles faintly. It does not trouble him much. If you want to dream of someone you love, it is good to lie alone like this for lengthy periods—no noise, no other people, in a bright, high-ceilinged room with treetops rustling outside. It is sweet to think everything over

in peace, dream gentle dreams of your love, undisturbed
by any arrangements and duties, alone and at your ease
with the tender dream images that approach the bed when
you close your eyes for a moment. Love may have no more
quietly beautiful moments than these pale, twilight dreams.

He still feels severe pain for the first few days, but it is
mingled with a curious kind of pleasure. The idea that he
has suffered this pain for the sake of his beloved Margot
gives the boy a highly romantic, almost ecstatic sense of
self-confidence. He wishes he had a wound, he thinks, a
blood-red injury to his face that he could have taken around
openly, all the time, like a knight wearing his lady's favours;
alternatively, it would have been good never to wake up
again at all but stay lying down there, broken to pieces
outside her window. His dream is already under way; he
imagines her awakened in the morning by the sound of
voices under her window, all talking together, sees her bending curiously down and discovering him—him!—shattered
there below the window, dead for her sake. He pictures her
collapsing with a scream; he hears that shrill cry in his ears,
and then sees her grief and despair as she lives on, sad and
serious all her life, dressed in black, her lips quivering faintly
when she is asked the reason for her sorrow.

He dreams like this for days, at first only in the dark,
then with open eyes, getting accustomed to the pleasant
memory of her dear image. Not an hour is so bright or
full of activity as to keep her picture from coming to him,
a slight shadow stealing over the walls, or her voice from
reaching his ears through the rippling rustle of the leaves

and the crunch of sand outside in the strong sunlight. He converses with Margot for hours like this, or dreams of accompanying her on their travels, on wonderful journeys. Sometimes, however, he wakes from these reveries distraught. Would she really mourn for him if he were dead? Would she even remember him?

To be sure, she sometimes comes in person to visit the invalid. Often, when he is talking to her in his mind and seems to see her lovely image before him, the door opens and she comes in, tall and beautiful, but so different from the being in his dreams. For she is not gentle, nor does she bend down with emotion to kiss his brow, like the Margot of his dreams; she just sits down beside his chaise longue, asks how he is and whether he is in any pain, and then tells him a few interesting stories. He is always so sweetly startled and confused by her presence that he dares not look at her; often he closes his eyes to hear her voice the better, drinking in the sound of her words more deeply, that unique music that will then hover around him for hours. He answers her hesitantly, because he loves the silence when he hears only her breathing, and is most profoundly alone with her in this room, in space itself. And then, when she stands up and turns to the door, he stretches and straightens up with difficulty, despite the pain, so that he can memorize the outline of her figure in movement, see her in her living form before she lapses into the uncertain reality of his dreams.

Margot visits him almost every day. But doesn't Kitty visit him too, and Elisabeth, little Elisabeth who always looks so startled, and asks whether he feels better yet in such kind tones of concern? Doesn't his sister come to see him daily, and the other women, and aren't they all equally kind to him? Don't they stay with him, telling him amusing stories? In fact they even stay too long, because their presence drives away his mood of reverie, rouses it from its meditative peace and forces him to make casual conversation and utter silly phrases. He would rather none of them came except for Margot, and even she only for an hour, only for a few minutes, and then he would be on his own again to dream of her undisturbed, uninterrupted, quietly happy as if buoyed up on soft clouds, entirely absorbed in the consoling images of his love.

So sometimes, when he hears a hand opening the door, he closes his eyes and pretends to be asleep. Then the visitors steal out again on tiptoe, he hears the handle quietly closing, and knows that now he can plunge back into the warm tide of his dreams gently bearing him away to enticingly faraway places.

And one day a strange thing happens: Margot has already been to visit him, only for a moment, but she brought all the scents of the garden in her hair, the sultry perfume of jasmine in flower, and the bright sparkling of the August sun was in her eyes. Now, he knew, he could not expect her again today. It would be a long, bright afternoon, shining with sweet reverie, because no one would disturb him; they had all gone riding. And when the door moves again, hesitantly, he squeezes his eyes shut, imitating sleep. However, the woman coming in—as he can clearly hear in the breathless stillness of the room—does not retreat, but closes the door without a sound so as not to wake him. Now she steals towards him, stepping carefully, her feet barely touching the floor. He hears the soft rustle of a dress, and knows that she is sitting down beside him. And through the crimson mist behind his closed eyelids, he feels that her gaze is on his face.

His heart begins to thud. Is it Margot? It must be. He senses it, but it is sweeter, wilder, more exciting, a secret, intriguing pleasure not to open his eyes yet but merely guess at her presence beside him. What will she do now? The seconds seem to him endless. She is only looking at him, listening to him sleeping, and that idea sends an electric tingling through his pores, the uncomfortable yet intoxicating sense of being vulnerable to her observation, blind and defenceless, to know that if he opened his eyes now they would suddenly, like a cloak, envelop Margot's startled face in tender mood. But he does not move, although his breath comes unsteadily from a chest too constricted for it, and he waits and waits.

Nothing happens. He feels as if she were bending down closer to him, as if he sensed, closer to his face now, her faint perfume, a soft, moist lilac scent that he knows from her lips. And now she has placed her hand on the chaise longue and is gently stroking his arm above the rug spread over him—the blood surges from that hand in a hot wave through his whole body—stroking his arm calmly and carefully. He feels that her touch is magnetic,

97

and his blood flows in response to it. This gentle affection, intoxicating and intriguing him at the same time, is a wonderful feeling.

Slowly, almost rhythmically, her hand is still moving along his arm. He peers up surreptitiously between his eyelids. At first he sees only a crimson mist of restless light, then he can make out the dark, speckled rug, and now, as if it came from far away, the hand caressing him; he sees it very, very dimly, only a narrow glimpse of something white, coming down like a bright cloud and moving away again. The gap between his eyelids is wider and wider now. He sees her fingers clearly, pale and white as porcelain, sees them curving gently to stroke forward and then back again, dallying with him, but full of life. They move on like feelers and then withdraw; and at that moment the hand seems to take on a life of its own, like a cat snuggling close to a dress, a small white cat with its claws retracted, purring affectionately, and he would not be surprised if the cat's eyes suddenly began to shoot sparks. And sure enough, isn't something blinking brightly in that white caress? No, it's only the glint of metal, a golden shimmer. But now, as the hand moves forward again, he sees clearly that it is the medallion dangling from her bracelet, that mysterious, giveaway medallion, octagonal and the size of a penny. It is Margot's hand caressing his arm, and a longing rises in him to snatch up that soft, white hand—it wears no rings—carry it to his lips and kiss it. But then he feels her breath, senses that Margot's face is very close to his, and he cannot keep his eyelids pressed together any longer. Happily, radiantly, he turns his gaze on the face now so close, and sees it retreat in alarm.

And then, as the shadows cast by the face bent down to him disperse and light shows her features, stirred by emotion, he recognizes—it is like an electric shock going through his limbs—he recognizes Elisabeth, Margot's sister, that strange girl young Elisabeth. Was this a dream? No, he is staring into a face now quickly blushing red, she is turning her eyes away in alarm, and yes, it is Elisabeth. All at once he guesses at the terrible mistake he has made; his eyes gaze avidly at her hand, and the medallion really is there on her bracelet.

Mists begin swirling before his eyes. He feels exactly as he did when he fainted after his fall, but he grits his teeth; he doesn't want to lose his ability to think straight. Suddenly it all passes rapidly before his mind's eye, concentrated into a single second: Margot's surprise and haughty attitude, Elisabeth's smile, that strange look of hers touching him like a discreet hand—no, there was no possible mistake about it.

He feels one last moment of hope, and stares at the medallion; perhaps Margot gave it to her, today or yesterday or earlier.

But Elisabeth is speaking to him. His fevered thinking must have distorted his features, for she asks him anxiously, "Are you in pain, Bob?"

How like their voices are, he thinks. And he replies only, without thinking, "Yes, yes… I mean no… I'm perfectly all right!"

There is silence again. The thought keeps coming back to him in a surge of heat: perhaps Margot has given it to her, and that's all. He knows it can't be true, but he has to ask her.

"What's that medallion?"

"Oh, a coin from some American republic or other, I don't know which. Uncle Robert gave it to us once."

"Us?"

He holds his breath. She must say it now.

"Margot and me. Kitty didn't want one, I don't know why."

He feels something wet flowing into his eyes. Carefully, he turns his head aside so that Elisabeth will not see the tear that must be very close to his eyelids now; it cannot be forced back, it slowly, slowly rolls down his cheek. He wants to say something, but he is afraid that his voice might break under the rising pressure of a sob. They are both silent, watching one another anxiously. Then Elisabeth stands up. "I'll go now, Bob. Get well soon." He shuts his eyes, and the door creaks quietly as it closes.

His thoughts fly up like a startled flock of pigeons. Only now does he understand the enormity of his mistake. Shame and anger at his folly overcome him, and at the same time a fierce pain. He knows now that Margot is lost to him for ever, but he feels that he still loves her, if not yet, perhaps, with a desperate longing for the unattainable. And Elisabeth—as if in anger, he rejects her image, because all her devotion and the now muted fire of her passion cannot mean as much to him as a smile from Margot or the touch of her hand in passing. If Elisabeth had revealed herself to him from the first he would have loved her, for in those early hours he was still childlike in his passion; but now, in his thousand dreams of Margot, he has burnt her name too deeply into his heart for it to be extinguished now.

He feels everything darkening before his eyes as his constantly whirling thoughts are gradually washed away by tears. He tries in vain to conjure up Margot's face in his mind as he has done in all the long, lonely hours and days of his illness; a shadow of Elisabeth always comes in front of it, Elisabeth with her deep, yearning eyes, and then he is in confusion and has to think again, in torment, of how it all happened. He is overcome by shame to think how he stood outside Margot's window calling her name, and again he feels sorry for quiet, fair-haired Elisabeth, for whom he never had a word or a look to spare in all these days, when his gratitude ought to have been bent on her like fire.

Next morning Margot comes to visit him for a moment. He trembles at her closeness, and dares not look her in the eye. What is she saying to him? He hardly hears it; the wild buzzing in his temples is louder than her voice. Only when she leaves him does he gaze again, with longing, at her figure. He feels that he has never loved her more.

Elisabeth visits him in the afternoon. There is a gentle familiarity in her hands, which sometimes brush against his, and her voice is very quiet, slightly sad. She speaks, with a certain anxiety, of indifferent things, as if she were afraid of giving herself away if she talked about the two of them. He does not know quite what he feels for her. Sometimes he feels pity for her, sometimes gratitude for her love, but he cannot tell her so. He hardly dares to look at her for fear of lying to her.

She comes every day now, and stays longer too. It is as if, since the hour when the nature of their shared secret dawned on them, their uncertainty has disappeared as well. Yet they never dare to talk about those hours in the dark of the garden.

One day Elisabeth is sitting beside his chaise longue again. The sun is shining brightly outside, a reflection of the green treetops in the wind trembles on the walls. At such moments her hair is as fiery as burning clouds, her skin pale and translucent, her whole being shines and seems airy. From his cushions, which lie in shadow, he sees her face smiling close to him, and yet it looks far away because it is radiant with light that no longer reaches him. He forgets everything that has happened at this sight. And when she bends down to him, so that her eyes seem to be more profound, moving darkly inward, when she leans forward he puts his arm round her, brings her head close to his and kisses her delicate, moist mouth. She trembles like a leaf but does not resist, only caresses his hair with her hand. And then she says, merely breathing the words, with loving sorrow in her voice, "But Margot is the only one you love." He feels that tone of devotion go straight to his heart, that gentle, unresisting despair, and the name that shakes him with emotion strikes at his very soul. But he dares not lie at that minute. He says nothing in reply.

She kisses him once more, very lightly, an almost sisterly kiss on the lips, and then she goes out without a word.

That is the only time they talk about it. A few more days, and then the convalescent is taken down to the garden, where the first faded leaves are already chasing across the path and early evening breathes an autumnal melancholy. Another few days, and he is walking alone with some difficulty, for the last time that year, under the colourful autumn canopy of leaves. The trees speak louder and more angrily now than on those three mild summer nights. The boy, in melancholy mood himself, goes to the place where they were once together. He feels as if an invisible, dark wall were standing here behind which, blurred in twilight already, his childhood lies; and now there is another land before him, strange and dangerous.

He said goodbye to the whole party that evening, looked hard once more at Margot's face, as if he had to drink enough of it in to last for the rest of his life, placed his hand restlessly in Elisabeth's, which clasped it with warm ardour, almost looked past Kitty, their friends and his sister—his heart was so full of the realization that he loved one of the sisters and the other loved him. He was very pale, with a bitter expression on his face that made him seem more than a boy; for the first time, he looked like a man.

And yet, when the horses were brought up and he saw Margot turn indifferently away to go back up the steps, and when Elisabeth's eyes suddenly shone with moisture, and she held the balustrade, the full extent of his new experience overwhelmed him so entirely that he gave himself up to tears of his own like a child.

The castle retreated farther into the distance, and through the dust raised by the carriage the dark garden looked smaller and smaller. Then came the countryside, and finally all that he had experienced was hidden from his eyes—but his memory was all the more vivid. Two hours of driving took him to the nearest railway station, and next morning he was in London.

A few more years and he was no longer a boy. But that first experience had left too strong an impression ever to fade. Margot and Elisabeth had both married, but he did not want to see them again, for the memory of those hours sometimes came back to him so forcefully that his entire later life seemed to him merely a dream and an illusion by comparison with its reality. He became one of those men who cannot find a way of relating to women, because in one second of his life the sensation of both loving and being loved had united in him entirely; and now no longing urged him to look for what had fallen into his trembling, anxiously yielding boyish hands so early. He travelled in many countries, one of those correct, silent Englishmen whom many consider unemotional because they are so reserved, and their eyes look coolly away from the faces and smiles of women. For who thinks that they may bear in them, inextricably mingled with their blood, images on which their gaze is always fixed, with an eternal flame burning around them as it does before icons of the Madonna? And now I remember how I heard this story. A card had been left inside the book that I was reading this afternoon, a postcard sent to me by a friend in Canada.

He is a young Englishman whom I met once on a journey. We often talked in the long evenings, and in what he said the memory of two women sometimes suddenly and mysteriously flared up, as if they were distant statues, and always in connection with a moment of his youth. It is a long time, a very long time since I spoke to him, and I had probably forgotten those conversations. But today, on receiving that postcard, the memory was revived, mingling dreamily in my mind with experiences of my own; and I felt as if I had read his story in the book that slipped out of my hands, or as if I had found it in a dream.

But how dark it is now in this room, and how far away you are from me in the deep twilight! I can see only a faint pale light where I think your face is, and I do not know if you are smiling or sad. Are you smiling because I make up strange stories for people whom I knew fleetingly, dream of whole destinies for them, and then calmly let them slip back into their lives and their own world? Or are you sad for that boy who rejected love and found himself all at once cast out of the garden of his sweet dream for ever? There, I didn't mean my story to be dark and melancholy—I only wanted to tell you about a boy suddenly surprised by love, his own and someone else's. But stories told in the evening all tread the gentle path of melancholy. Twilight falls with its veils, the sorrow that rests in the evening is a starless vault above them, darkness seeps into their blood, and all the bright, colourful words in them have as full and heavy a sound as if they came from our inmost hearts.

THE DEBT PAID LATE

M Y DEAR ELLEN,
I know you will be surprised to receive a letter from me after so long; it must be five or perhaps even six years since I last wrote to you. I believe that then it was a letter of congratulations on your youngest daughter's marriage. This time the occasion is not so festive, and perhaps my need to confide the details of a strange encounter to you, rather than anyone else, may strike you as odd. But I can't tell anyone else what happened to me a few days ago. You are the only person who would understand.

My pen involuntarily hesitates as I write these words, and I have to smile at myself a little. Didn't we exchange the very same "You are the only person who would understand" a thousand times when we were fifteen or sixteen years old—immature, excitable girls telling each other our childish secrets at school or on the way home? And didn't we solemnly swear, long ago in our salad days, to tell each other everything, in detail, concerning a certain person? All that is more than a quarter of a century ago; but a promise, once made, must be kept. And as you will see, I am faithfully keeping my word, if rather late in the day.

This was how it all happened. I have had a difficult and strenuous time of things this year. My husband was appointed medical director of the big hospital in R., so I had all the complications of moving house to deal with; meanwhile my son-in-law went to Brazil on business, taking my daughter with him, and they left their three children in our house. The children promptly contracted scarlet fever one after the other, and I had to nurse them... and that wasn't all, because then my mother-in-law died. Everything was happening at once. I thought at first that I had survived all these headlong events pretty well, but somehow they must have taken more out of me than I knew, because one day my husband said, after looking at me in silence for some time, "Margaret, I think that now the children, thank goodness, are better again you ought to do something about your own health. You look overtired, you've been well and truly overdoing things. Two or three weeks at a sanatorium in the country, and you'll be your old self again."

My husband was right. I was exhausted, more so than I admitted to myself. I became aware of it when I realized that in company—and since my husband took up his post here, there have been many functions to host and many calls to be paid—after an hour I couldn't concentrate properly on what people were saying, while I forgot the simplest things more and more often in the daily running of the household, and had to force myself to get up in the morning. With his observant and medically trained eye, my husband had diagnosed my physical and mental weariness correctly. All I really needed was two weeks to recover.

Fourteen days without thinking about the meals, the laundry, paying calls, doing all the everyday business—fourteen
days on my own to be myself, not a mother, grandmother,
housekeeper and wife of the medical director of a hospital
all the time. It so happened that my widowed sister was
available to come and stay, so everything was prepared
for my absence; and I had no further scruples in follow-
ing my husband's advice and going away by myself for
the first time in twenty-five years. Indeed, I was actually
looking forward quite impatiently to being invigorated by
my holiday. I rejected my husband's suggestion only in
one point: his idea that I should spend it at a sanatorium,
although he had thoughtfully found one whose owner had
been a friend of his from their youth. But there would
have been other people whom I knew there, and I would
have had to go on being sociable and mixing in company.
All I really wanted was to be on my own for fourteen days
with books, walks, time to dream and sleep undisturbed,
fourteen days without the telephone and the radio, fourteen
days of silence at peace with myself, if I may put it like
that. Unconsciously, I hadn't wanted anything so much for
years as this time set aside for silence and rest.

And then I remembered that in the first years of my
marriage, when my husband was practising as an assistant
doctor in Bolzano, I had once spent three hours walking
up to an isolated little village high in the mountains. In
its tiny marketplace, opposite the church, stood one of
those rural inns of the kind so often to be found in the
Tyrol, its ground floor built of massive stones, the first

floor under the wide, overhanging wooden roof opening on to a spacious veranda, and the whole place surrounded by vine leaves that in autumn, the season when I saw it, glowed around the whole house like a red fire gradually cooling. Small outbuildings and big barns huddled to the right and left of it, but the house itself stood on its own under soft autumnal clouds drifting across the sky, and looked down at the endless panorama of the mountains.

At the time I had felt almost spellbound outside that little inn, and I wanted to go in. I'm sure you know what it's like to see a house from the train or on a walk, and think all of a sudden: oh, why don't I live here? I could be happy in this place. I think such an idea occurs to everyone sometimes, and when you have looked at a house for a long time secretly wishing to live happily in it, everything about it is imprinted on your memory. For years I remembered the red and yellow flowers growing in window boxes, the wooden first-floor gallery, where laundry was fluttering like colourful banners the day I saw it, the painted shutters at the windows, yellow on a blue background with little heart-shapes cut out of the middle of them, and the roof ridge with a stork's nest on the gable. When my heart felt restless I sometimes thought of that house. How nice it would be to go there for a day, I would think, in the dreamy, half-unconscious way that you think of something impossible. And now wasn't this my best chance to make my old, and by this time almost forgotten, wish come true? Wasn't the prettily painted house on the mountainside, an inn without the tiresome amenities of our modern world, with no telephone or radio, the very thing for overtired nerves? I would have no visitors there, and there would be no formalities. As I called it to mind again, I thought I was breathing in the strong, aromatic mountain air, and hearing the far-off ringing of rustic cowbells. Even remembering it gave me fresh courage and made me feel better. It was one of those ideas that take us by surprise apparently for no reason at all, although in reality they express wishes that we have cherished for a long time, waiting in the unconscious mind. My husband, who didn't know how often I had dreamt of that little house, seen only once years ago, smiled a little at first but promised to make enquiries. The proprietors replied that all of their three guest rooms were vacant at the moment, and I could choose whichever I liked. All the better, I thought, no neighbours, no conversations; and I went on the night train. Next morning, a little country one-horse trap took me and my small suitcase up the mountain at a slow trot.

It was all as delightful as I could have hoped for. The room was bright and neat, with its simple, pale pine furniture, and from the veranda, which was all mine in the absence of any other guests, I had a view into the endless distance. A glance at the well-scoured kitchen, shining with cleanliness, showed me, experienced housewife that I am, that I would be very well looked after here. The landlady, a thin, friendly, grey-haired Tyrolean, assured me again that I need not fear being disturbed or pestered by visitors. True, the parish clerk, the local policeman and a few of the other neighbours came to the inn every evening to drink a glass or so, play cards and talk. But they were all quiet folk, and at eleven they went home again. On Sunday after church, and sometimes in the afternoon, the place was rather livelier, because the locals came to the inn from their farms or the mountains; but I would hear hardly any of that in my room.

The day was too bright and fine, however, for me to stay indoors for long. I unpacked the few things I had brought, asked for a piece of good brown country bread and a couple of slices of cold meat to take out with me, and went walking over the meadows, climbing higher and higher. The landscape lay before me, the valley with its fast-flowing river, the surrounding snow-crowned peaks, as free as I was myself. I felt the sun on every pore of my skin, and I walked and walked and walked for an hour, two hours, three hours until I reached the highest Alpine meadows. There I lay down to rest, stretched out on the soft, warm moss, and felt a wonderful sense of peace come over me, together with the buzzing of the bees, the light and rhythmic sound of the wind—it was exactly what I had been longing for. I closed my eyes pleasurably, fell to dreaming, and didn't even notice when at some point I dropped off to sleep. I was woken only by a chill in the air on my limbs. Evening was coming on, and I must have slept for five hours. Only now did I realize how tired I had been. But I had good, fresh air in my nerves and in my bloodstream. It took me only two hours to walk back to the little inn with a strong, firm, steady step.

The landlady was standing at the door. She had been slightly anxious, fearing I might have lost my way, and offered to prepare my supper at once. I had a hearty appetite and was hungrier than I could remember feeling for years, so I was very happy to follow her into the main room of the inn. It was not large—a dark, low-ceilinged room with wood-panelled walls, very comfortable with its red-and-blue check tablecloths, the chamois horns and crossed shotguns on the walls. And although the big blue-tiled stove was not heated this warm autumn day, there was a comfortable natural warmth inside the room. I liked the guests as well. At one of the four tables the local police-man, the customs officer and the parish clerk sat playing cards together, each with a glass of beer beside him. A few farmers with strong, sun-browned faces sat at their ease at another, propping their elbows on it. Like all Tyroleans, they said little, and merely puffed at their long-stemmed porcelain pipes. You could see that they had worked hard all day and were relaxing now, too tired to think, too tired to talk—honest, upright men; it did one good to look at their faces, as strongly outlined as woodcuts. A couple of carters occupied the third table, drinking strong grain schnapps in small sips, and they too were tired and silent. The fourth table was laid for me, and soon bore a portion of roast meat so huge that normally I wouldn't have managed to eat half of it; but I had a healthy, even ravenous appetite after walking in the fresh mountain air.

I had brought a book down, meaning to read, but it was pleasant sitting here in this quiet room, among friendly people whose proximity was neither oppressive nor a nuisance. Sometimes the door opened, a fair-haired child came to fetch a jug of beer for his parents, or a farmer dropped in and emptied a glass standing at the bar. A woman came for a quiet chat with the landlady, who sat behind the bar darning socks for her children or grand-children. There was a wonderful quiet rhythm to all this coming and going, which offered something for my eyes to see and was no burden on my heart, and I felt very well in such a comfortable atmosphere.

I had been sitting dreamily like that for a while, think-ing of nothing in particular, when—it will have been about nine o'clock—the door was opened again, but not this time in the slow, unhurried way of the locals. It was suddenly flung wide, and the man who came in stood for a moment on the threshold filling the doorway, as if not quite sure whether to come in. Only then did he let the door latch behind him, much more loudly than the other guests, look around the room and greet all present with a deep-voiced and resonant, "A very good evening to you one and all, gentlemen!" I was immediately struck by his rather ornate and artificial vocabulary. In a Tyrolean vil-lage inn, people do not usually greet the "gentlemen" with such ceremony, and in fact this rather ostentatious form of address seemed to meet with an unenthusiastic response from the other guests in the room. No one looked up, the landlady went on darning grey woollen socks, and one of the carters was the only person to grunt an indifferent "Evening" in return, but in a tone of voice suggesting, "And to the devil with you!" No one seemed surprised by the strange guest's manner, but he was not to be deterred by this unforthcoming reception. Slowly and gravely, he hung up his broad hat with its well-worn brim—not a rustic item of headgear—on one of the chamois horns, and then looked from table to table, not sure where to sit down. Not a word of welcome came from any of them. The three card-players immersed themselves with conspicuous concentration in their game, the farmers on their benches gave not the slightest sign of moving closer to make room, and I myself, made to feel rather uncomfortable by the stranger's manner and fearing that he might turn out to be talkative, was quick to open my book.

So the stranger had no choice but to go over to the bar with a noticeably heavy, awkward step. "A beer, if mine hostess pleases, as fresh and delicious as your lovely self," he ordered in quite a loud voice. Once again I was struck by his dramatically emotional tone. In a Tyrolean village inn, such an elaborately turned compliment seemed out of place, and there was nothing whatsoever about that kindly old grandmother the landlady to justify it. As was to be expected, such a form of address failed to impress her. Without replying, she picked up one of the sturdy stoneware tankards, rinsed it out with water, dried it with a cloth, filled it from the barrel and pushed it to the newcomer over the bar, in a manner that was not exactly discourteous but was entirely indifferent.

Since the round paraffin lamp hung from its chains above him, right in front of the bar, I had a chance to take a better look at this unusual guest. He was about sixty-five years old, was very stout, and with the experience I had gained as a doctor's wife I immediately saw the reason for the dragging, heavy gait that I had noticed as soon as he came into the room. A stroke must have affected one side of his body to some extent, for his mouth also turned down on that side, and the lid of his left eye visibly drooped lower than his right eyelid. His clothes were out of place for an Alpine village; instead of the countryman's rustic jacket and lederhosen, he wore baggy yellow trousers that might once have been white, with a coat that had obviously grown too tight for him over the years and was alarmingly shiny at the elbows; his tie, carelessly arranged, hung from his fleshy, fat neck like a piece of black string. There was something run-down about his appearance in general, and yet it was possible that this man had once cut an imposing figure. His brow, curved and high, with thick, untidy white hair above it, had something of a commanding look, but just below his bushy eyebrows the decline set in: his eyes swam under reddened lids; his slack, wrinkled cheeks merged with his soft, thick neck. I was instinctively reminded of the mask of a late Roman emperor that I had once seen in Italy, one of those who presided over the fall of Rome. At first I did not know what it was that made me observe him so attentively, but I realized at once that I must take care not to show my curiosity, for it was obvious that he was already impatient to strike up a conversation with someone. It was as if he were under some compulsion to talk. As soon as he had raised his glass in a slightly shaky hand and taken a sip, he exclaimed in a loud voice, "Ah, wonderful, wonderful!" and looked around him. No one responded. The card-players shuffled and dealt the pack, the others smoked their pipes; they all seemed to know the new arrival and yet, for some reason of which I was unaware, not to feel any curiosity about him.

Finally there was no restraining him any longer. Picking up his glass of beer, he carried it over to the table where the farmers were sitting. "Will you gentlemen make a little room for my old bones?" The farmers moved together slightly and took no further notice of him. For a while he said nothing, pushing the half-full glass alternately forwards and backwards. Once again, I saw that his fingers trembled. Finally he leant back and began talking, in quite a loud voice. It was not really obvious whom he was addressing, for the two rustics sitting next to him had clearly shown that they were disinclined to embark on any conversation. He was, in fact, addressing everyone at large. He spoke—I sensed that at once—in order to speak and to hear himself speaking.

"Well, what a business that was today!" he began. "Well-meant of the Count, well-meant, I grant you. Meets me while he's driving along the road and stops his car, yes, indeed, he stops it specially for me. He's taking his children down to Bolzano to go to the cinema, says he, how would I like to go with them? Well, he's a distinguished man, a cultured, educated man, the Count knows where respect is due, and you don't say no lightly to such a man, not if you know what's right. So I go along with them, in the back seat of course, with his lordship the Count—after all, it's an honour, a man like that, and I let him take me into that magic-lantern show they've opened in the high street with such a fuss, advertisements and lights fit for a church festival. Well, I think, why shouldn't I see what those gentlemen the British and Americans are churning out over there, selling the stuff to us for good money? It's said to be quite an art, this cinema acting. Shame on them, say I"—and here he spat copiously—"shame on them for the rubbish they show on that screen of theirs! It's a disgrace to art, a disgrace to a world that has a Shakespeare and a Goethe in it! First came all that coloured nonsense with comical animals—well, I'll say nothing about that, it may be fun for children, it does no one any harm. But then they make a film of *Romeo and Juliet*—now that ought to be forbidden, forbidden in the name of art! The lines sound as if someone was croaking them into a stovepipe, those sacred lines of Shakespeare's, and all so sugary and sentimental! I'd have got up and walked out if I hadn't been there with his lordship the Count, on his invitation. Making such rubbish out of pure refined gold! And to think that we live in times like these!"

He grasped his glass of beer, took a large draught and put it down with a loud bang. His voice was very loud now, he was almost shouting. "And that's what actors do these days—they spit out Shakespearian lines into machines for money, filthy lucre, dragging their art in the dirt! Give me any tart in the street—I have more respect for her than for those apes with their smooth faces metres wide on the posters, raking in millions for committing a crime against art! Mutilating the word, the living word, shouting Shakespeare's verse into a funnel instead of edifying the public, instead of educating young people. A moral institution, that's what Schiller called the theatre, but that doesn't hold good any more. Nothing holds good any more but money, filthy money, and the spectacle they make of themselves. And anyone who doesn't know how to do that will die. Better die, say I—in my eyes, those who sell themselves to that sink of iniquity, Hollywood, should go to the gallows. To the gallows with them, I say, to the gallows!"

He had been shouting at the top of his voice and thumping the table with his fist. One of the trio at the card-players' table growled, "Keep quiet, can't you? We can't tell what cards we're playing through your stupid gabbling!"

The old man gave a start, as if to reply. For a moment there was strength and vigour in his dull gaze, but then he merely made a contemptuous gesture, as much as to imply that it was beneath him to answer. The two farmers beside him puffed at their pipes, and he stared silently ahead with glazed eyes, saying nothing, his expression sombre. You could tell it was not the first time he had forced himself to hold his tongue.

I was deeply shaken, and felt a pang. Something stirred in me at the sight of this humiliated man, who I felt at once must have seen better days, and yet somehow had sunk so low, perhaps because of drink. I could hardly breathe for fear that he or the others might embark on a violent scene. From the first moment when he came in and I had heard his voice, something in him—I didn't know what—had made me uneasy. But nothing happened. He sat still, his head sinking lower, he stared ahead, and I felt as if he were muttering something quietly to himself. No one took any more notice of him.

Meanwhile, the landlady had got up from the bar to fetch something from the kitchen. I took that as a chance to follow her and ask who the man was. "Oh," she said, unruffled, "poor fellow, he lives in the poorhouse here, and I give him a beer every evening. He can't afford to pay for it himself. But we don't have an easy time with him. He used to be an actor once somewhere or other, and it hurts his feelings that people don't really believe he ever amounted to much and show him no respect. Sometimes they poke fun at him, asking him to put on a show for them. Then he stands up and spouts stuff that nobody understands for hours. Sometimes they give him some tobacco for his pains, or buy him another beer. Sometimes they just laugh at him, and then he loses his temper. You have to go carefully with him, but he wouldn't hurt a fly. Two or three beers if someone will pay for them, and then he's happy—yes, poor devil, there's no harm in old Peter."

"What—what is his name?" I asked, startled without knowing why.

"Peter Sturzentaler. His father was a woodcutter in the village here, so they took him in at the poorhouse."

Well, my dear, you can imagine what had startled me so much. For at once I understood what might seem unimaginable. This Peter Sturzentaler, this down-at-heel, drunk, sick old man from the poorhouse, could be none other than the idol of our young days, the master of our dreams; the man who as Peter Sturz the actor, the male lead in our city theatre, had been the quintessence of all that was elevated and sublime, whom as you will remember, both of us—young girls who were still half children—had admired so madly, loved to such distraction. And now I also knew why something in the first words he spoke on entering the inn had troubled me. I had not recognized him—how could I have recognized him behind this mask of debasement, in such a state of change and decay?—but there had been something in his voice that found its way to my long-buried memory. Do you remember when we first saw him? He had come from some provincial city when our municipal theatre in Innsbruck offered him an engagement, and it so happened that our parents said we could go to the performance introducing him to Innsbruck audiences because it was a classic play, Grillparzer's *Sappho*, and he was playing the part of Phaon, the handsome young man who creates turmoil in Sappho's heart. But remember how he captured ours when he came on stage, in Greek costume, a wreath in his thick, dark hair, a new Apollo! He had hardly spoken his first lines before we were both trembling with excitement and holding hands with each other. We had never seen a man like this in our dull, sedate city of Innsbruck, and the young provincial actor, whose stage make-up and the artifice of whose presentation could not be seen from the gallery, seemed to us a divine symbol of all that was noble and sublime. Our foolish little hearts beat fast in our young breasts; we were different girls when we left the theatre, enchanted, and as we were close friends and did not want to endanger our friendship, we swore to each other to love and venerate him together. That was the moment when our madness began. Nothing mattered to us except him. All that happened at school, at home, in town was mysteriously linked with him, everything else paled beside him; we gave up loving books, and the only music we wanted to hear was in his voice. I think we talked of nothing else for months on end. Every day began with him; we hurried downstairs to get to the newspaper before our parents, to know what new part he had been given, to read the reviews; and none of them was enthusiastic enough for us. If there was a critical remark about him we were in despair, we hated any other actor who won praise. Oh, we committed too many follies for me to be able to remember a thousandth part of them today. We knew when he went out, and where he was going, we knew whom he spoke to, and envied everyone who could stroll down the street with him. We knew the ties he wore, the stick he carried; we hid photographs of him not only at home but inside the covers of our school textbooks, so that we could take a secret look at him in the middle of lessons; we had invented our own secret language so that at school we could signal, from desk to desk, that he was in our thoughts. A finger raised to the forehead meant, "I'm thinking of him now." When we had to read poems aloud, we instinctively imitated his voice, and to this day I can hardly see many of the plays in which I first saw him without hearing the lines spoken in his voice. We waited for him at the stage door and followed him, we stood in the entrance of a building opposite the café that he patronized, and watched endlessly as he read the newspaper there. But our veneration for him was so great that in those two years we never dared to speak to him or try to get to know him personally. Other, more uninhibited girls who also admired him would beg for his autograph, and even dared to address him in the street. We never summoned up the courage for that. But once, when he had thrown away a cigarette end, we picked it up as if it were a holy relic and divided it in two, half for you and half for me. And this childish idolatry was transferred to everything that had any connection with him. His old housekeeper, whom we envied greatly because she could serve him and look after him, was an object of our veneration too. Once, when she was shopping in the market, we offered to carry her basket for her, and were glad of the kind words she gave us in return. Ah, what folly wouldn't we have committed for Peter Sturz, who neither knew nor guessed anything about it?

Today, now that we have become middle-aged and therefore sensible people, it may be easy for us to smile scornfully at our folly as the usual rapturous fantasy of a girlish adolescent crush. And yet I cannot conceal from myself that in our case it had already become dangerous. I think that our infatuation took such absurd, exaggerated shape only because, silly children that we were, we had sworn to love him together. That meant that each of us tried to outdo the other in her flights of fancy, and we egged each other on further every day, thinking of more and more new evidence to prove that we had not for a moment forgotten the idol of our dreams. We were not like other girls, who by now were swooning over smooth-cheeked boys and playing silly games; to us, all emotion and enthusiasm was bent on this one man. For those two passionate years, all our thoughts were of him alone. Sometimes I am surprised that after this early obsession we could still love our husbands and children later with a clear-minded, sound and healthy love, and we did not waste all our emotional strength in those senseless excesses. But in spite of everything, we need not be ashamed of that time. For, thanks to the object of our love, we also lived with a passion for his art, and in our folly there was still a mysterious urge towards higher, purer, better things; they acquired, purely by coincidence, personification in him.

All this already seemed so very far away, overgrown by another life and other feelings; and yet when the landlady told me his name, it gave me such a shock that it is a miracle she didn't notice it. It was so startling to meet the man whom we had seen only surrounded by the aura of our infatuation, had loved so wholeheartedly as the very emblem of youth and beauty, and to find that he was a beggar now, the recipient of anonymous charity, a butt of the mockery of simple-minded peasants and already too old and tired to feel ashamed of his decline—so startling that it was impossible for me to go back into the main room of the inn. I might not have been able to restrain my tears at the sight of him, or I might have given myself away to him by some other means. I had to regain my composure first. So I went up to my room to think, to recollect clearly what this man had meant to me in my youth. The human heart is strange: for years and years I had not given him a single thought, although he had once dominated all my thoughts and filled my whole soul. I could have died and never asked what had become of him; he could have died and I would not have known.

I did not light a lamp in my room, I sat in the dark, trying to remember both the beginning and the end of it all; and all at once I seemed to be back in that old, lost time. I felt as if my own body, which had borne children many years ago, was a slender, immature girl's body again, and I was the girl who used to sit on her bed with her heart beating fast, thinking of him before she went to sleep. Involuntarily, I felt my hands turn hot, and then something happened that alarmed me, something that I can hardly describe to you. A shudder suddenly ran through me, and at first I did not know why. Something shook me severely. A thought, a certain thought, a certain memory had come back to me; it was one that I had shut out of my mind for years and years. At the very second when the landlady told me his name, I felt something within me lying heavily on my mind, demanding expression, something that I didn't want to remember, something that, as that Professor Freud in Vienna says, I "had suppressed"—had suppressed at such a deep level that I really had forgotten it for years on end, one of those profound secrets that one defiantly keeps even from oneself. I also kept it from you at the time, even after swearing to tell you everything I knew about him. I had hidden it from myself for years. Now it had been roused and was close to the surface of my mind again; and only now that it is for our children, and soon our grandchildren, to commit their own follies, can I confess to you what happened between me and that man at the time.

And now I can tell you my most intimate secret openly. This stranger, this old, broken, down-at-heel actor who would now deliver lines of verse in front of the local rustics for a glass of beer, and was the object of their laughter and contempt—this man, Ellen, held my whole life in his hands for the space of a dangerous minute. If he had taken advantage of that moment—and it was in his power to do so—my children would never have been born, and I do not know where or what I would have been today. The friend who is writing you this letter today would probably have been an unhappy woman, and might have been as crushed and downtrodden by life as he was himself. Please don't think that I exaggerate. At the time, I myself did not understand the danger I was in, but today I see and understand clearly what I did not understand at the time. Only today do I know how deeply indebted I was to that stranger, a man I had forgotten.

I will tell you about it as well as I can. You will remember that at the time, just before your sixteenth birthday, your father was suddenly transferred from Innsbruck, and I can still see you in my mind's eye weeping stormily in my room, sobbing out the news that you would have to leave me—and leave *him*. I don't know which was harder for you. I am inclined to believe that it was the fact that you would lose sight of him, the idol of our youth, without whom life seemed to you not worth living. You made me swear to tell you everything about him, write you a letter every week, no, every day, write a whole diary—and for some time I faithfully did it. It was hard for me to lose you, too, because whom could I confide in now, to whom could I describe the emotional high flights and blissful folly of my exuberant feelings? However, I still had him, I could see him, he was mine and only mine now; and in the midst of my pain there was a little pleasure in that. But soon afterwards—as you may have heard—there was an incident that we knew only in vague outline. It was said that Sturz had made advances to the wife of the manager of the theatre—at least, so I was told later—and after a violent scene he had been forced to accept dismissal. He was allowed one final benefit performance. He was to tread the boards of our theatre once more, and then I too would have seen him for the last time.

Thinking back to it today, I don't believe that any other day in my life was unhappier than the one when it was announced that Peter Sturz would be on stage in Innsbruck for the last time. I felt ill. I had no one to share my desperation with, no one to confide in. At school the teachers noticed how distracted and disturbed I looked; at home I was so violent and frantic that my father, guessing nothing, lost his temper and forbade me, on pain of punishment, to go to the theatre. I pleaded with him—perhaps too hard and too passionately—and only made matters worse, because my mother too now spoke against

me, saying all that theatre-going had been a strain on my
nerves and I must stay at home. At that moment I hated
my parents—yes, I was so confused and deranged that
day that I hated them and couldn't bear the sight of them.
I locked myself into my room. I wanted to die. One of
those sudden fits of melancholy that can actually endanger
young people now and then overcame me; I sat rigid in
my chair, I did not shed any tears—I was too desperate for
that. Sometimes all was cold as ice inside me, and then I
would suddenly feel feverish and go from room to room.
I flung the window up and stared down at the yard three
storeys below, assessing how far I would fall if I jumped
out. And again and again my eyes went to my watch: it
was only three in the afternoon, and the performance
began at seven. He was going to act in our theatre for the
last time, and I wouldn't hear him; everyone else would
cheer him to the echo, and I wouldn't be there. Suddenly
I couldn't bear it any more. I ignored my parents' prohibi-
tion on my leaving the house. I went out without a word
to anyone, downstairs and out into the street—I don't
know where I thought I was going. I believe I had some
confused notion of drowning myself or doing something
else senseless. I just didn't want to live any more without
him, and I did not know how to put an end to my life.
And so I went up and down the streets, ignoring friends
when they hailed me. I was indifferent to everything, no
one else in the world existed for me, he was the only one.
Suddenly, I don't know how it happened, I was standing
outside the building where he lived. You and I had often

waited in the entrance to the building opposite to see if he might come home, or we looked up at his windows, and perhaps that vague hope of meeting him by chance some time had unconsciously driven me here. But he did not appear. Dozens of unimportant people, the postman, a carpenter, a fat woman from the market, left the building or went into it, hundreds and hundreds of people who didn't matter to me hurried past in the street; but he never put in an appearance.

I don't remember how the next part happened, but suddenly I felt drawn there. I crossed the road, went up the stairs to the second floor without stopping to get my breath back, and then went to the door of his apartment; I just had to be close to him, nearer to him! I had to say something to him, although I didn't know what. I really was in a state of possession by a madness that I couldn't account for to myself, and perhaps I ran up the stairs so fast in order to outrun any kind of circumspect thought. I was already—still without stopping for breath—pressing the doorbell. I can hear its high, shrill note to this day, and then there was a long wait in total silence, broken suddenly by the sound of my awakening heart. At last I heard footsteps inside: the firm, heavy tread I knew from his appearances at the theatre. And at that moment sober reflection returned to me. I wanted to run away from the door again, but everything in me was frozen in alarm. My feet felt paralysed, and my little heart stood still.

He opened the door and looked at me in surprise. I don't know if he knew or recognized me at all. Out in the street there were always dozens of his immature admirers, boys and girls alike, flocking around him. But the two of us who loved him most had been too shy, we had always fled rather than meet his eyes. And this time, too, I stood before him with my head bent, and dared not look up. He waited to hear what I had to say to him—he obviously thought I was an errand girl from one of the shops in town bringing him a message. "Well, my child, what is it?" he finally encouraged me in his deep, sonorous voice.

I stammered, "I only wanted to… but I can't say it here…" And I stopped again.

He said in a kindly tone, "Well, come in, then, child. What's it about?"

I followed him into his room. It was a large, simple place, rather untidy; the pictures had already been taken down from the walls, cases were standing around half-packed. "There now, tell me… who sent you here?" he asked again.

And suddenly it came bursting out of me in a torrent of burning tears. "Please stay here… please, please don't go away… stay here with us."

He instinctively took a step back. His brows shot up, and his mouth tightened in a sharp line. He had realized that I was another of those importunate admirers who kept pestering him, and I was afraid he would say something angry. But there must have been something about me that made him take pity on my childish despair. He came up to me and gently patted my arm: "My dear child,"—he spoke like a teacher addressing a pupil—"it's not my own doing that I am leaving this place, and it can't be altered now. It

132

is very nice of you to come and ask me to stay. Who do we actors perform for if not the young? It has always been a particular joy to me if young people applaud us. But the die is cast, and I can't do anything about that. Well, as I said,"—and he stepped back again—"it was very, very nice of you to come and tell me what you have, and I thank you. Be a good girl, and I hope you will all think of me kindly."

I realized that he had said goodbye, but that only increased my desperation. "No, stay here," I exclaimed, sobbing, "for God's sake, stay here... I... I can't live without you."

"My dear child," he said soothingly, but I clung to him, clung to him with both arms—I who had never before had the courage even to brush against his coat. "No, don't go away," I went on, still sobbing in despair, "don't leave me alone! Take me with you. I'll go anywhere you like with you... anywhere... do what you like to me... only don't leave me."

I don't know what other nonsensical stuff I poured out in my despair. I pressed close to him as if I could keep him there like that, with no idea at all of the dangerous situation my passionate outburst was inviting. You know how naive we still were at the time, and what a strange and unknown idea physical love was to us. But I was a young girl and—I can say so today—a strikingly pretty girl; men were already turning in the street to look at me, and he was a man, thirty-seven or thirty-eight years old at the time. He could have done anything he liked to me; I really would have followed him, and whatever he had tried I would have offered no resistance. It would have been easy for him to take advantage of my ignorance there in his apartment. At that moment my fate was in his hands. Who knows what would have become of me if he had improperly abused my childish persistence, if he had given way to his vanity, and perhaps his own desires and the strength of temptation? Only now do I understand what danger I was in. There was a moment at which, I now feel, he was not sure of himself, when he sensed my body pressed to his, and my quivering lips were very close. But he controlled himself and slowly pushed me away. "Just a moment," he said, breaking free of me almost by force, and he turned to the other door. "Frau Kilcher!"

I was horrified. Instinctively, I wanted to run away. Was he going to hold me up to ridicule in front of his old housekeeper? Make fun of me in front of her? Then she came in, and he turned to her. "What do you think, Frau Kilcher," he said to her, "this young lady has come to bring me warm farewell wishes in the name of her whole school. Isn't that touching?" He turned to me again. "Please tell your friends I am very grateful. I have always felt that the beauty of our profession is having youth, and thus the very best thing there is on earth, on our side. Only young people appreciate the finer points of the stage, I assure you, only they. You have given me great pleasure, my dear young lady, and"—here he clasped my hands—"I will never forget it."

My tears dried up. He had not shamed me, he had not humiliated me. But his concern for me went even further, because he turned to his housekeeper again: "Well, if we didn't have so much to do, I would very much have liked to talk to this charming young lady for a little while. However, you will escort her down to the door, Frau Kilcher, won't you? My very good wishes to you, my very good wishes."

Only later did I realize how thoughtful of him it was to spare and protect me by sending the housekeeper down to the door of the building with me. After all, I was well known in the little city of Innsbruck, and some ill-disposed person might have seen me, a young girl, stealing out of the famous actor's apartment all by myself, and could have spread gossip. Although he was a stranger to me, he understood better than I, still a child, what endangered me. He had protected me from my own ignorant youth—how clear that was to me now, more than twenty-five years later.

Isn't it strange, my dear friend, doesn't it put me to shame that I had forgotten all that for years and years, because I was so ashamed that I *wanted* to forget it? That I had never felt truly grateful to this man, never asked after him, when he had held my life, my fate in his hands that afternoon? And now the same man was sitting downstairs over his glass of beer, a wreck of a failure, a beggar, despised by everyone; no one knew who he was and who he had been except for me. I was the only one aware of it. Perhaps I was the only person on earth who still remembered his name, and I was indebted to him. Now I might be able to repay my debt. All at once I felt very calm. I was no longer upset, only a little ashamed of my injustice in forgetting, for so long, that this stranger had once been generous to me at a crucial moment in my life.

I went downstairs and back into the main room of the
inn. I suppose that only some ten minutes in all had passed.
Nothing had changed. The card game was still going on,
the landlady was at the bar, doing her mending, the local
rustics were sleepily puffing their pipes. He too was still sitting in his place, with his empty glass in front of him, staring
ahead. Only now did I see how much sorrow there was in
that wreck of a face, his eyes dull under their heavy lids, his
mouth grim and bitter, distorted by the stroke. He sat there
gloomily with his elbows on the table so that he could prop
his bowed head in his hands, warding off his weariness.
It was not the weariness of sleep; he was tired of life. No
one spoke to him, no one troubled about him. He sat there
like a great grey bird with tattered feathers, crouching in
its cage, perhaps dreaming of its former freedom when it
could still spread its wings and fly through the air.

The door opened again and three more of the locals
came in, with heavy, dragging footsteps, ordered their beer
and then looked around for somewhere to sit. "Move up,
you," one of them ordered him rather brusquely. Poor
Sturz looked up. I could see that the rough contempt with
which they treated him hurt his feelings. But he was too
tired and humiliated by now to defend himself or dispute
the point. He moved aside in silence, pushing his empty
beer glass along with him. The landlady brought full
tankards for the newcomers. He looked at them, I noticed,
with an avid, thirsty glance, but the landlady ignored his
silent plea with composure. He had already had his charity
for that evening, and if he didn't leave then that was his

136

fault. I saw he no longer had the strength of mind to stand up for himself, and how much more humiliation awaited him in his old age!

At that moment the liberating idea occurred to me at last. I couldn't really help him, I knew that. I couldn't make a broken, worn-out man young again. But perhaps I could give him a little protection against the pain of such contempt, retrieve a little esteem for him in this village at the back of beyond for the few months he had left to live, already marked as he was by the finger of Death.

So I stood up and walked over, making something of a show of it, to the table where he was sitting squeezed between the locals, who looked up in surprise at my arrival, and addressed him. "Do I by any chance have the honour of speaking to Herr Sturz, leading man at the Court Theatre?"

He started in surprise. It was like an electric shock going right through him; even the heavy lid over his left eye opened. He stared at me. Someone had called him by his old name, known to no one here, by the name that all except for him had long ago forgotten, and I had even described him as leading man at the Court Theatre, which in fact he never had been. The surprise was too great for him to summon up the strength to get to his feet. Gradually, his gaze became uncertain; perhaps this was another joke thought up by someone in advance.

"Well, yes… that is… that was my name."

I offered him my hand. "Oh, this is a great pleasure for me… and a really great honour." I was intentionally raising my voice, because I must now tell outright lies to get him some respect in this company. "I must admit that I have never had the good fortune of admiring you on stage myself, but my husband has told me about you again and again. He often saw you at the theatre when he was a schoolboy. I think it was in Innsbruck…"

"Yes, Innsbruck. I was there for two years." His face suddenly began coming to life. He realized that I was not setting out to make fun of him.

"You have no idea, Herr Sturz, how much he has told me, how much I know about you! He will be so envious when I write tomorrow to tell him that I was lucky enough to meet you here in person. You can't imagine how much he still reveres you. No other actor, not even Kainz, could equal you, he has often told me, in the parts of Schiller's Marquis of Posa and Max Piccolomini, or as Grillparzer's Leander; and I believe that later he went to Leipzig just to see you on stage there. But he couldn't pluck up the courage to speak to you. However, he has kept all your photographs from those days, and I wish you could visit our house and see how carefully they are treasured. He would be delighted to hear more about you, and perhaps you can help me by telling me something more about yourself that I can pass on to him… I don't know whether I am disturbing you, or whether I might ask you to join me at my table."

The rustics beside him stared, and instinctively moved respectfully aside. I saw that they were feeling both uneasy and ashamed. They had always treated this old man as a beggar to be given a beer now and then and used as a laughing stock. But observing the respectful manner that I, a total stranger, adopted towards him, they were overcome for the first time by the unsettling suspicion that he was well known and even honoured out in the wider world. The deliberately humble tone that I assumed in requesting the favour of a conversation with him was beginning to take effect. "Off you go, then," the farmer next to him urged.

He stood up, still swaying, as you might stand up on waking from a dream. "By all means... happily," he stammered. I realized that he had difficulty in restraining his delight, and that as a former actor he was now wrestling with himself in an effort not to show the others present how surprised he was, and taking great pains, if awkwardly, to behave as if such requests, accompanied by such admiration, were everyday matters to be taken for granted. With the dignity acquired in the theatre, he strode slowly over to my table.

"A bottle of wine," I ordered, "the best you have in the house, in honour of Herr Sturz of the Court Theatre." Now the card-players also looked up from their game and began to whisper. Their old acquaintance Sturzentaler a famous man who used to act at the Court Theatre? There must be something about him if this strange woman from the big city showed him such respect. And it was in a different manner that the landlady now set a glass down in front of him.

Then he and I passed a wonderful hour. I told him everything I knew about him by pretending that I had heard it from my husband. He could hardly contain his amazement at finding that I could enumerate every one of the parts he had taken at Innsbruck, the name of the theatre critic there, and every word that critic had written about him. And then I quoted the incident when Moissi, the famous actor Moissi, after giving a guest performance, had declined to come out to the front of the stage to receive the applause alone, but had made Sturz join him, addressing him in fraternal fashion. Again and again, he expressed his astonishment as if in a dream. "You know about that, too!" He had thought his memory dead and buried long ago, and now here came a hand knocking on its coffin, taking it out, and conjuring up for him fame of a kind that he never really had. But the heart is always happy to lie to itself, and so he believed in that fame of his in the world at large, and suspected nothing. "You even know that… why, I had forgotten it myself," he kept stammering, and I noticed that he had difficulty in not showing his emotion; two or three times he took a large and rather grubby handkerchief out of his coat pocket and turned away as if to blow his nose, but really to wipe away the tears running down his wrinkled cheeks. I saw that, and my heart shook to see that I could make him happy, I could give this sick old man one more taste of happiness before his death.

So we sat together in a kind of rapture until eleven o'clock. At that point the police officer came deferentially up to the table to point out courteously that by law it was closing time. The old man was visibly startled; was this heaven-sent miracle coming to an end? He would obviously have liked to sit here for hours hearing about himself, dreaming of himself. But I was glad of the official warning, for I kept fearing that he must finally guess the truth of the matter. So I asked the other men, "I hope you gentlemen will be kind enough to see Herr Sturz of the Court Theatre safely home."

"With the greatest pleasure," they all said at the same time; one of them respectfully fetched him his shabby hat, another helped him up, and I knew that from now on they would not make fun of him, laugh at him or hurt the feelings of this poor old man who had once been such a joy to us, such a necessity in our youth.

As we said goodbye, however, the dignity he had maintained at some expense of effort deserted him, emotion overwhelmed him, and he could not preserve his composure. Large tears suddenly streamed from his tired old eyes, and his fingers trembled as he clasped my hand. "Ah, you good, kind, gracious lady," he said, "give your husband my regards, and tell him old Sturz is still alive. Maybe I can return to the theatre some day. Who knows, who knows, I may yet recover my health."

The two men supported him on his right and left, but he was walking almost upright; a new pride had straightened the broken man's back, and I heard a different note in his voice. I had been able to help him at the end of his life, as he had helped me at the beginning of mine. I had paid my debt.

Next morning I made my excuses to the landlady, saying that I could not stay any longer; the mountain air was too strong for me. I tried to leave her money to give the poor old man a second and third glass of beer whenever he wanted it, instead of that single tankard. But here I came up against her own native pride. No, she would do that herself anyway. They hadn't known in the village that Sturzentaler had been such a great man. It was an honour to the village as a whole, the mayor had already decided that he should be paid a monthly allowance, and she herself would vouch for it that they would all take good care of him. So I merely left a letter for him, a letter of effusive thanks for his kindness in devoting an evening to me. I knew he would read it a thousand times before his death, and show the letter to everyone; he would blissfully dream the false dream of his own fame again and again before his end.

My husband was greatly surprised to see me back from my holiday so soon, and even more surprised to find how happy and reinvigorated those two days away had left me. He described it as a miracle cure. But I see nothing miraculous about it. Nothing makes one as healthy as happiness, and there is no greater happiness than making someone else happy.

There—and now I have also paid my debt to you from the days when we were girls. Now you know all about Peter Sturz, our idol, and you know the last, long-kept secret of

Your old friend
Margaret.

FORGOTTEN DREAMS

T HE VILLA LAY CLOSE TO THE SEA.
   The quiet avenues, lined with pine trees, breathed
out the rich strength of salty sea air, and a slight breeze
constantly played around the orange trees, now and then
removing a colourful bloom from flowering shrubs as if
with careful fingers. The sunlit distance, where attractive houses built on hillsides gleamed like white pearls,
a lighthouse miles away rose steeply and straight as a
candle—the whole scene shone, its contours sharp and
clearly outlined, and was set in the deep azure of the sky
like a bright mosaic. The waves of the sea, marked by
only the few white specks that were the distant sails of
isolated ships, lapped against the tiered terrace on which
the villa stood; the ground then rose on and on to the
green of a broad, shady garden and merged with the rest
of the park, a scene drowsy and still, as if under some
fairy-tale enchantment.

Outside the sleeping house on which the morning heat
lay heavily, a narrow gravel path ran like a white line to
the cool viewing point. The waves tossed wildly beneath
it, and here and there shimmering spray rose, sparkling

in rainbow colours as brightly as diamonds in the strong sunlight. There the shining rays of the sun broke on the small groups of Vistulian pines standing close together, as if in intimate conversation, they also fell on a Japanese parasol with amusing pictures on it in bright, glaring colours, now open wide.

A woman was leaning back in a soft basket chair in the shade of this parasol, her beautiful form comfortably lounging in the yielding weave of the wicker. One slender hand, wearing no rings, dangled down as if forgotten, petting the gleaming, silky coat of a dog with gentle, pleasing movements, while the other hand held a book on which her dark eyes, with their black lashes and the suggestion of a smile in them, were concentrating. They were large and restless eyes, their beauty enhanced by a dark, veiled glow. Altogether the strong, attractive effect of the oval, sharply outlined face did not give the natural impression of simple beauty, but expressed the refinement of certain details tended with careful, delicate coquetry. The apparently unruly confusion of her fragrant, shining curls was the careful construction of an artist, and in the same way the slight smile that hovered around her lips as she read, revealing her white teeth, was the result of many years of practice in front of the mirror, but had already become a firmly established part of the whole design and could not be laid aside now.

There was a slight crunch on the sand.

She looks without changing her position, like a cat lying basking in the dazzling torrent of warm sunlight and merely blinking apathetically at the newcomer with phosphorescent eyes.

The steps quickly come closer, and a servant in livery stands in front of her to hand her a small visiting card, then stands back a little way to wait.

She reads the name with that expression of surprise on her features that appears when you are greeted in the street with great familiarity by someone you do not know. For a moment, small lines appear above her sharply traced black eyebrows, showing how hard she is thinking, and then a happy light plays over her whole face all of a sudden, her eyes sparkle with high spirits as she thinks of the long-ago days of her youth, almost forgotten now. The name has aroused pleasant images in her again. Figures and dreams take on distinct shape once more, and become as clear as reality.

"Ah, yes," she said as she remembered, suddenly turning to the servant, "yes, of course show the gentleman up here."

The servant left, with a soft and obsequious tread. For a moment there was silence except for the never-tiring wind singing softly in the treetops, now full of the heavy golden midday light.

Then vigorous, energetic footsteps were heard on the gravel path, a long shadow fell at her feet, and a tall man stood before her. She had risen from her chair with a lively movement.

Their eyes met first. With a quick glance he took in the elegance of her figure, while a slight ironic smile came

147

into her eyes. "It's really good of you to have thought of me," she began, offering him her slender and well-tended hand, which he touched respectfully with his lips.

"Dear lady, I will be honest with you, since this is our first meeting for years, and also, I fear, the last for many years to come. It is something of a coincidence that I am here; the name of the owner of the castle about which I was enquiring because of its magnificent position recalled you to my mind. So I am really here under false pretences."

"But nonetheless welcome for that, and in fact I myself could not remember your existence at first, although it was once of some significance to me."

Now they both smiled. The sweet, light fragrance of a first youthful, half-unspoken love, with all its intoxicating tenderness, had awoken in them like a dream on which you reflect ironically when you wake, although you really wish for nothing more than to dream it again, to live in the dream. The beautiful dream of young love that ventures only on half-measures, that desires and dares not ask, promises and does not give.

They went on talking. But there was already a warmth in their voices, an affectionate familiarity, that only a rosy if already half-faded secret like theirs can allow. In quiet words, broken by a peal of happy laughter now and then, they talked about the past, or forgotten poems, faded flowers, lost ribbons—little love tokens that they had exchanged in the little town where they spent their youth. The old stories that, like half-remembered legends, rang bells in their hearts that had long ago fallen silent, stifled by dust, were slowly, very slowly invested with a melancholy solemnity; the final notes of their youthful love, now dead, brought profound and almost sad gravity to their conversation.

His darkly melodious voice shook slightly as he said, "All that way across the ocean in America, I heard the news that you were engaged—I heard it at a time when the marriage itself had probably taken place."

She did not reply to that. Her thoughts were ten years back in the past. For several long minutes, a sultry silence hung in the air between them.

Then she asked, almost under her breath, "What did you think of me at the time?"

He looked up in surprise. "I can tell you frankly, since I am going back to my new country tomorrow. I didn't feel angry with you, I had no moments of confused, hostile indecision, since life had cooled the bright blaze of love to a dying glow of friendship by that time. I didn't understand you—I just felt sorry for you."

A faint tinge of red flew to her cheeks, and there was a bright glint in her eyes as she cried, in agitation, "Sorry for me! I can't imagine why."

"Because I was thinking of your future husband, that indolent financier with his mind always bent on making money—don't interrupt me, I really don't mean to insult your husband, whom I always respected in his way—and because I was thinking of you, the girl I had left behind. Because I couldn't see you, the independent idealist who had only ironic contempt for humdrum everyday life, as the conventional wife of an ordinary person."

"Then why would I have married him if it was as you say?"

"I didn't know exactly. Perhaps he had hidden qualities that escaped a superficial glance and came to light only in the intimacy of your life together. And I saw that as the easy solution to the riddle, because one thing I could not and would not believe."

"And that was?"

"That you had accepted him for his aristocratic title of Count and his millions. That was the one thing I considered impossible."

It was as if she had failed to hear those last words, for she was looking through her fingers, which glowed deep rose like a murex shell, staring far into the distance, all the way to the veils of mist on the horizon where the sky dipped its pale-blue garment into the dark magnificence of the waves.

He too was lost in thought, and had almost forgotten that last remark of his when, suddenly and almost inaudibly, she turned away from him and said, "And yet that is what happened."

He looked at her in surprise, almost alarm. She had settled back into her chair with slow and obviously artificial composure, and she went on in a soft melancholy undertone, barely moving her lips.

"None of you understood me when I was still a girl, shy and easily intimidated, not even you who were so close to me. Perhaps not even I myself. I think of it often now, and I don't understand myself at that time, because what do women still know about their girlish hearts that believed in miracles, whose dreams are like delicate little white flowers that will be blown away at the first breath of reality? And I was not like all the other girls who dreamt of virile, strong young heroes who would turn their yearnings into radiant happiness, their quiet guesses into delightful knowledge, and bring them release from the uncertain, ill-defined suffering that they cannot grasp, but that casts its shadow on their girlhood, becoming more menacing as it lies in wait for them. I never felt such things, my soul steered other dreams towards the hidden grove of the future that lay behind the enveloping mists of the coming days. My dreams were my own. I always dreamt of myself as a royal child out of one of the old books of fairy tales, playing with sparkling, radiant jewels, wearing sweeping dresses of great value—I dreamt of luxury and magnificence, because I loved them both. Ah, the pleasure of letting my hands pass over trembling, softly rustling silk, or laying my fingers down in the soft, darkly dreaming pile of a heavy velvet fabric, as if they were asleep! I was happy when I could wear jewels on my slender fingers as they trembled with happiness, when pale gemstones looked out of the thick torrent of my hair, like pearls of foam; my highest aim was to rest in the soft upholstery of an elegant vehicle. At the time I was caught up in a frenzied love of artistic beauty that made me despise my real, everyday life. I hated myself in my ordinary clothes, looking simple and modest as a nun, and I often stayed at home for days on end because I was ashamed of my humdrum appearance, I hid myself in my cramped, ugly room, and my dearest dream was to live alone beside the sea, on a property both magnificent and artistic, in shady, green garden walks that were never touched by the dirty hands of the common workaday world, where rich peace reigned—much like this place, in fact. My husband made my dreams come true, and because he could do that I married him."

She has fallen silent now, and her face is suffused with Bacchanalian beauty. The glow in her eyes has become deep and menacing, and the red in her cheeks burns more and more warmly.

There is a profound silence, broken only by the monotonous rhythmical song of the glittering waves breaking on the tiers of the terrace below, as if casting itself on a beloved breast.

Then he says softly, as if to himself, "But what about love?"

She heard that. A slight smile comes to her lips.

"Do you still have all the ideals, *all* the ideals that you took to that distant world with you? Are they all still intact, or have some of them died or withered away? Haven't they been torn out of you by force and flung in the dirt, where thousands of wheels carrying vehicles to their owners' destination in life crushed them? Or have you lost none of them?"

He nods sadly, and says no more.

Suddenly he carries her hand to his lips and kisses it in silence. Then he says, in a warm voice, "Goodbye, and I wish you well."

She returns his farewell firmly and honestly. She feels no shame at having unveiled her deepest secret and shown her soul to a man who has been a stranger to her for years. Smiling, she watches him go, thinks of the words he said about love, and the past comes up with quiet, inaudible steps to intervene between her and the present. And suddenly she thinks that *he* could have given her life its direction, and her ideas paint that strange notion in bright colours.

And slowly, slowly, imperceptibly, the smile on her dreaming lips dies away.

PUSHKIN PRESS

Pushkin Press was founded in 1997. Having first rediscovered European classics of the twentieth century, Pushkin now publishes novels, essays, memoirs, children's books, and everything from timeless classics to the urgent and contemporary.

Pushkin Paper books, like this one, represent exciting, high-quality writing from around the world. Pushkin publishes widely acclaimed, brilliant authors such as Stefan Zweig, Antoine de Saint-Exupéry, Antal Szerb, Paul Morand and Hermann Hesse, as well as some of the most exciting contemporary and often prize-winning writers, including Pietro Grossi, Héctor Abad, Filippo Bologna and Andrés Neuman.

Pushkin Press publishes the world's best stories, to be read and read again.

*